Everyone who'd been standing around—talking and waiting for the meeting to begin—shuffled closer, jockeying for a better view. And that's when I noticed him.

Sean Reed.

"Oh, my gosh," Liz whispered harshly beside me. "Do you see—"

"I see."

"How are they even letting *him* be a CIT?" she asked. "That is so not fair!"

As usual, she was totally reading my mind.

XOXOXOXO

Read all the FIRST KISSES books:

FIRST KISSES

Trust Me

Rachel Hawthorne

HarperTempest

An Imprint of HarperCollins*Publishers*

HarperTempest is an imprint of
HarperCollins Publishers.

www.harperteen.com

Library of Congress Catalog Card Number:
2006928092
ISBN-10: 0-06-114308-1
ISBN-13: 978-0-06-114308-3

Typography by Andrea Vandergrift

First HarperTempest edition, 2007

For every girl
who has dreamed of that first kiss

XOXOX

Trust
Me

Chapter One

XOXOX

"What were we thinking?" Liz asked.

I'll admit it had been my brilliant idea. As a matter of fact, most of *our* ideas started out as *my* brilliant idea.

It's not that my best friend, Liz, isn't creative. She is. She's incredibly artsy, especially when it comes to craft projects. She made the shoulder bags that we carried around at school. Mine was pink with fringe and sequins. Hers was blue with felt-shaped puppies on it. They actually started a trend, and for a while she had a business going. She also created a lot of the jewelry I wear: earrings, bracelets, necklaces. She always makes them kinda whimsical: a lady in a flowing gown sitting on a crescent moon, a unicorn. Stuff like that. Real originals. So Liz is definitely creative.

But the idea to rearrange the furniture in our dormitory was definitely mine.

"We were thinking that four beds lined up along one wall looked like something from the mental ward in a psycho movie," I reminded her. Maybe we'd been a bit harsh with our original assessment of our surroundings. Maybe it more closely resembled an army dormitory. Which I figured was fitting since we were basically at boot camp. Counselors' boot camp.

Anyway, I'd suggested we shove the beds so each one was angled out from a corner of the room.

"Now we have something from *Charmed*," Liz said. "All we need is a pentagram in the middle . . ." Her voice trailed off and she released a tiny giggle. "Bad, bad idea, Jess." She giggled again. "I mean, it just doesn't . . . work."

I started laughing and fell back on the bed. It wasn't often that my ideas didn't work. The problem with this one was that one of the beds angled in a corner blocked the door to the bathroom. So yeah, it definitely wasn't going to work.

"Okay," I said. "For now, let's just put everything back the way it was."

I got up and started pushing my bed back against the far wall, while Liz started pushing hers.

We had spent the past four summers coming to Camp Lone Star. In the past, we'd been designated as nothing more than campers, having a great time, goofing around, working on the craft projects that Liz was so good at, telling scary stories while sitting around the campfire, becoming friends with kids from other schools in the area. Last summer, our favorite pastime had become checking out the guys and rating them according to cuteness factor.

But this year we wanted to do more than

follow orders. We wanted to be the ones issuing orders. And we wanted to do more than check and rate the guys. We wanted to seriously connect with them. And one of the things that our previous observations had shown us was that guys tended to gravitate toward the counselors. Since Liz and I were now old enough, we'd applied to be those all-attention-getting counselors.

And we'd both been selected!

I was totally psyched!

Of course, the first step in being a counselor was attending leadership boot camp—"a week of intense team building," according to the letter we'd received announcing our selection as counselors. Not that I thought either of us needed leadership training. My younger brother, Alex, was always telling me that I was way too bossy. So I figured I'd be a natural at this job. Since Liz and I tended to excel at the same things, I was convinced she, too, would make an excellent counselor.

Our parents had dropped us off almost an hour ago, with the usual hugs, tears, and promises to call, to be careful, and to have fun. We wouldn't see our parents for almost a month, a week longer than we'd ever been gone before, since the summer camping sessions were divided into three-week intervals. Strange how a month seemed so much longer than three weeks. But I had Liz and she had me, so we knew we'd survive the longer separation from our families. No problem.

We'd registered, received our uniforms, and headed to the dormitory. We'd put our gear in the footlockers at—you guessed it!—the foot of the beds. Then we'd decided to do the extreme room makeover. Now we had everything back to the way it was. Boring. Maybe when the other two girls we'd be sharing the room with arrived we could come up with another arrangement.

"Guess we'd better get ready for our first"— Liz wiggled her fingers, making quotation marks in the air—"official team meeting."

"Yeah, we don't want to be late for that."

Quickly we got dressed in our "official" camp counselor uniforms. Then we stared at each other. The clothes didn't exactly come from the Gap. They looked like they'd been made with the "one size fits all" approach.

"This is so not going to work," Liz said.

As usual Liz spoke out loud exactly what I was thinking. I wasn't sure if she could read my mind because she'd been my best friend forever or if she'd been my best friend forever because she could read my mind.

"I don't remember the counselors wearing *anything* that looked like this," Liz said. She swept her hand from her head to her narrow hips, like a sorcerer about to cast a spell that might rid her of what she was wearing.

"Maybe these are just our 'in training' clothes," I offered hopefully.

"Jess, they stitched our names over the pocket. That's a lot of trouble for something we'll wear for only a week."

Good point. Above my left pocket was stitched in red JESSICA KANE. Above Liz's was ELIZABETH STEWART. I didn't know anyone who called her Elizabeth. Not even her parents. At least mine called me Jessica.

But that wasn't the worst part. The worst was the baggy brown shorts. They looked like something my granddad wore with white socks and sandals when he walked the grounds at the assisted-living facility. And the shirt matched in all ways possible: color, bagginess, hideousness. Could the outfit get any more out of control?

Liz and I had sorta thought that this summer, the summer before we entered high school, would be the summer of transforming ourselves into guy magnets. But no way was that going to happen with our present clothing. It was like wearing a sign—WARNING: LOSER CROSSING.

I'll admit that in addition to becoming a guy magnet, I wanted to be a counselor because they were totally cool. They knew everything. They were the ones people turned to in a crisis. Like last year when the canoe I was in tipped over because the guys who'd also been in it had been goofing around, it was a counselor who helped get us all safely back to shore. They were the ones who decided our indoor activities—Did we play games like Twister or did we string beads or create artwork using leaves?—and our outdoor adventures—hiking, plant-life identification, trail marking, swimming. They had total control.

As much as I loved camp, the previous summers I'd experienced a few moments when I'd felt totally out of control. And very uncool. Thanks to one Sean Reed. We lived in the same large town north of Dallas but didn't attend the same middle school—although our schools flowed into the same high school so our paths might cross more often in the near future—something I was definitely not looking forward to. Anyway, in the past, we sorta had that school rivalry thing going. At least, I think that's what started his let-me-see-what-I-can-do-to-irritate-her shenanigans. From there it had escalated into obvious can't-stand-the-ground-she-walks-on dislike.

He'd gone so far as to nickname me Twinkle Toes the first summer. Simply because he'd spotted me sitting alone on the dock at the lake painting my toenails bright red. According to him, toenail polish shouldn't be anywhere near hiking boots. As though he would know.

Last summer he'd said I was like Paris Hilton. (But, trust me, I don't look anything like her!) Just because, one evening, some of the girls in our cabin had decided to have a makeover session. And all right—it had been another one of my brilliant ideas. But after two weeks of hiking, bugs, and "roughing it," I was more than ready for a little pampering. And so were they!

And I'll admit that we had gone totally extreme on the makeup and hair and nail polish. But we'd never planned for anyone outside our dormitory to see us. And no one would have if the guys hadn't decided it would be wicked hilarious to make us think a bear was trying to get in through our bathroom window. We'd all run out the front door, screaming for help.

The guys had laughed and snickered for days.

"There aren't any bears in these woods," Sean had announced, like we'd been totally stupid for falling for their gag.

If Sean Reed showed up at camp this year, I planned to assign him toilet-scrubbing duty. We'd see who was laughing then. Yep, this year I'd be totally in control. It was going to be the funnest summer yet!

"Okay," I said to Liz now. "This is fixable."

Do you consider yourself adaptable?

Question five on the application I'd completed in hopes of being selected as a counselor. I hadn't hesitated one sec before using my number-two pencil to shade in the oval next to the *Yes*.

I knelt beside the footlocker where I'd put my things shortly after we arrived. I pulled out a red camisole and waved it at Liz. "Find something red that matches the stitching, so we're at least color coordinated."

"Do you think it's okay for us to alter our clothing?"

All right, so maybe Liz wasn't leadership material just yet. I was usually the one with the ideas, and she always had to make sure we weren't going to get into trouble—or at least she wanted good odds that we weren't going to get caught. I didn't blame her. Her mom's two favorite words were "You're grounded," for the smallest of infractions. Like once, during a sleepover at Liz's house, our friend Joanie brought over the DVD of *Brokeback Mountain*. We're all huge Heath Ledger fans. Unfortunately, Liz's mom came into the room while we were watching the movie. Liz isn't allowed to watch R-rated movies. So she was grounded for a week. Getting away from the grounding machine was one of the reasons that Liz loved summer camp. The worst that happened here was an hour in the "jail."

"Do you really want to go out there looking like the UPS delivery guy?"

"Good point." She knelt beside her footlocker and began scrounging around. "I spent a lot of time looking at Cute Casey last year, and I sure don't remember him wearing this."

Cute Casey had been one of the counselors last summer. He was tall with dark hair, and looked exactly like this guy in an Abercrombie ad. He was way older than us—way out of our league, of course—but that was okay. If we were honest with ourselves, he was another reason—a major reason actually—that we wanted to be counselors this summer. Counselors had a later curfew than campers. After we all were supposed to be in bed, we could hear the counselors outside our dorms laughing and talking, just loud enough to be heard but not understood. They had secrets and we wanted to be part of their secrets.

Another reason was Gorgeous George. He had shaggy blond hair and blue, blue eyes. We didn't want either one of them to view us as kids any longer.

"Maybe we didn't notice what they were wearing because we were too busy studying their faces," I said. I pulled out a scarf that had red, white, and blue swirling through it. Talk about patriotic. I could use it as a belt.

"They?" Liz asked.

"Cute Casey and Gorgeous George."

"Oh, right, and don't forget Hot Hank."

It was a game we'd played last year, identifying the counselor with a word that began with his name. We'd done the same thing with the girl counselors, but we weren't nearly as complimentary. Crazy Claire—she hated the outdoors and was always finding reasons for us to have to stay indoors. It was crazy to come to Camp Lone Star if you didn't like the outdoors because the only time we were indoors during the day was when it rained. Moaning Mary—she moaned about the heat, the rain, the bugs. Patient Paula—she was never in a hurry, which meant if you got her for a counselor, you were the last in line for everything.

It wasn't that we didn't like them or tried to find fault with them, but they were competition. And I have kind of a competitive nature. The girl counselors held the attention of the guy counselors a lot more easily than lowly campers did.

This summer would be totally different. We would be sure of it. For one thing, we would be counselors. For another, we'd come better prepared. We'd brought these cute American Eagle visors, lots of short tops, and low-riding jeans and shorts.

It didn't take us long to add some flair to our outfits. Liz wore a red tank beneath her brown shirt, while I wore the camisole. We'd unbuttoned the shirts, gathered the shirttails, and tied them at our waist. Then we'd rolled up our shorts until they were mid-thigh.

"When we have more time, we'll have to cut and hem these babies," Liz said. "I'm so not going to start high school in the fall with a half-tanned leg."

"I know. This uniform is the worst. It still needs major surgery." And we could only take accessorizing so far. "Remember the crafts we did with beads last summer?" I asked.

"Absolutely! Are you thinking—"

"We could cut the sleeves into strips—"

"Braid the strips—"

"Thread them through the beads. Add some color, some pizzazz."

"I like it!" we both said at the same time, following our mind-reading session.

"Think we can do it before we head to the meeting?" Liz asked.

I glanced at my watch. It was actually my dad's, on loan for the summer. It was really way too big for my narrow wrist, but Dad had punched extra holes in the wristband so it wouldn't slip off. It had all kinds of gadgets. A compass—he worried about me getting lost in the woods. A face that lit up with the flick of my wrist—he worried about me getting lost in the dark. A button that would take me through the various time zones, just in case I ended up in London or Australia and needed to know the time. *As if.*

"We have only a couple of minutes before we need to report." I looked in the mirror that was on the back of the door that led into the bathroom. "I think we have a fashion statement going here that'll do for now."

I'd gathered my strawberry-blond hair into a ponytail and pulled it through the hole at the back of the brown baseball cap that had CLS embroidered in red on the front. I really wanted to toss the hat into my footlocker and grab my visor, but I figured we were pushing the limits on rebellion enough already.

Liz had also pulled her red hair through the back of her cap. She was several inches taller than me. Most people are. I tried not to be bothered by that, but sometimes I couldn't help it. I wished I was taller.

White socks and hiking boots completed our outfits.

"Are we ready to rock?" I asked.

"As ready as we'll ever be," Liz said.

Chapter Two

XOXOX

We headed out the door. Towering oak trees circled the encampment. I could smell the scent of dirt and dampness and vegetation—nature as a whole. Several wooden cabins made up the camp. The main building was where registration took place. The nurse's station was also located inside. Then a couple of cabins where the campers were housed had been built nearby. A lead counselor slept in each cabin, to be on hand for emergencies or homesickness and to keep campers indoors after lights-out.

Liz and I were Counselors-in-Training. Otherwise known as CITs. We'd live in the dormitory with other CITs. Which was fine with me. I didn't particularly want to look after a dozen kids through the night. I was hoping to spend some of the evening looking after my love life.

Speaking of . . .

I pulled my cell phone out of my shorts pocket. Its display was flashing, NO SIGNAL.

"Still no luck?" Liz asked.

"Nope. I wonder why we never realized that cell phones couldn't get a signal out here," I stated.

"Maybe because we never had cell phones before."

We'd both recently turned fourteen, me two weeks before Liz. We'd both asked for the same thing for our birthday. Cell phones. Big surprise. Having the ability to constantly keep in touch with our friends was such a must. Text messaging was also the absolute best, and we had the code down long before we could put it to use.

I'd had visions of text messaging a guy

counselor, "U R 2 CUTE." *Yeah, right, like I'd ever be that bold.*

My vast experience at communicating with guys mostly involved my brother, who was six years younger than me. Our conversations usually began with him whining, "I'm gonna tell Mom."

And my witty response: "Whatever."

I needed to seriously develop my flirtation skills—like figuring out what guys found interesting and what they wanted to talk about—and my brother was so not good practice material.

"Maybe once we go hiking, get farther away from camp, I'll be able to pick up a signal," I suggested hopefully, although I was beginning to suspect that the camp had been built in the one place that the Verizon-can-you-hear-me-now? guy had yet to visit.

Liz shook her head. "We're in the middle of nowhere. We should have expected this."

Or as my dad said, we were "on the *far*side of nowhere," which he seemed to think was worse than being in the middle of nowhere. I sorta figured nowhere was nowhere and it didn't have map coordinates. You were just there. No where.

"I think I'm going into cell phone withdrawal," I said, only half jokingly. My dad had constantly teased me for the last couple months that my hand was permanently curled in cell-phone-holding position. Of course, he said Mom's hand was permanently curled in credit-card-holding position.

"I'm already there," Liz said. Her phone wasn't getting a signal either.

Even though Liz was the person I called most, and we would be side by side most of the summer, we'd planned to use our phones for communicating on the sly.

QT 2 R = *Cutie to the right.*

QT 2 L = *Cutie to the left.*

I angled the phone and snapped a picture of Liz. At least the camera still worked. My dad was all about gadgets. No way was he going to get me a plain old cell phone for my birthday. Like my dad, I saw the value in multifunctional products. I intended to take lots of pictures, so bringing the cell phone along wasn't a total waste.

As Liz and I approached the main office building, we spotted a group of people milling around in front. Judging by their uniforms, they were all CITs. None were the counselors from last year, although I did recognize some people who had been campers during previous summers. I guess everyone had the idea of moving up to better things.

"I wonder where Cute Casey is," Liz whispered.

I shrugged. "He's already trained. Maybe this week it's just the newbies."

"Right." She scowled.

I watched her freckles scrunch up. With red hair comes freckles. When we were a lot younger—and really bored—we would use a Sharpie to connect the freckles on her arms to create pictures. So whenever I looked at her cheek really closely now, I always saw a kite that I'd drawn by connecting freckles. Actually, kites were pretty much all I'd ever seen and drawn. It's fairly easy to see a kite in freckles. Does that make me unimaginative?

I didn't want to contemplate that it might, since being a counselor meant coming up with creative ways to keep the campers occupied and away from the boredom zone.

"But if the older counselors aren't here, who's going to train us?" Liz asked me. Obviously her scowl had represented her thinking face.

"I'm sure someone will."

"Hey!" A couple of girls had turned, noticed us, and hurried over. We'd met them last summer. Caryn and Torie—Victoria, according to the name embroidered on her shirt. They'd shared a cabin with us and participated in our makeover session.

We didn't have much time to catch up on the exciting things we'd done since last summer—which was fine with me, since I'd done very little that I would classify as exciting. Now that I was actually here, I was beginning to have doubts that I could be an amazing counselor. Could I lead? Could I keep the campers entertained? Could I protect and serve . . .

oh, wait, that was the job of the police. Could I care for and console those who got homesick?

I was pretty sure I could, but soon I'd be tested.

Liz, Caryn, Torie, and I teased each other about the fact that none of us had kept our promise to stay in touch through e-mail or instant messaging. School has a way of taking up your time.

"I don't remember the counselors wearing these uniforms," Liz said. She was still hung up on not being entirely fashionable. Although trekking through the woods has a fashion of its own.

"Last year it was T-shirts," Caryn said. "I guess they wanted something a little classier."

"Classier?" Liz asked. "You think this is classier?"

"No, but I guess they thought it looked better than T-shirts."

"Maybe we'll get T-shirts after we finish this week of training," Torie said. "You know what I'm saying?"

"I liked T-shirts on the guy counselors," I admitted.

"Especially on Cute Casey," Liz said. "Anyone know if he's going to be here this year?"

Before anyone could answer, a clanging began. An iron triangle hung off the porch of the main lodge. Whenever our attention was needed, someone banged its insides with an iron rod. Our adventure camp had a rustic feel to it. While we had electricity, the bulbs always seemed to burn dimly. The TV in the dining hall, where we all gathered if we wanted to watch any television shows, was a very small screen and not high-def. The reception was lousy. No satellite dish. It did have a VHS tape player, but it wasn't exactly modern.

A woman—the tallest woman I'd ever seen, and her blond hair was practically buzzed— stood on the porch beside a man whose long dark hair was held in place with a leather tie. Excitement hummed on the air. In front of them stood four counselors I recognized from last year. Unfortunately, there wasn't a Casey,

Hank, or George among them. I wondered what happened to those guys. They'd probably been the oldest of the crew, and it seemed like they'd been around forever. Surely they hadn't moved on to other things. Like college or the army or a real job.

Everyone who'd been standing around — talking and waiting for the meeting to begin — shuffled closer, jockeying for a better view. And that's when I noticed him.

Sean Reed.

"Oh, my gosh," Liz whispered harshly beside me. "Do you see—"

"I see."

"How are they even letting *him* be a CIT?" she asked. "That is so not fair!"

As usual, she was totally reading my mind.

XOXOX

Chapter Three

S ean Reed. My arch-nemesis. Four years running. And it looked like we were going to make it five. He couldn't be a CIT. Absolutely couldn't be.

But he was wearing the uniform. And he was standing in the midst of the crowd, waiting to hear whatever *She* and *He* standing on the porch had to say.

The first year we'd met Sean, we'd rated him a nine out of a possible ten. But that was before we really got to know him. His ranking quickly descended to zero for a variety of reasons, including some dumb pranks that involved flying mashed potatoes during supper our first summer here. He was an absolute loser, although it wasn't apparent just looking at him. You had to get really close to him to see beyond the dark hair and the blue eyes and the killer smile.

Against my better judgment, I angled my head slightly to get a better look at him. Something about him was different. Was he a little taller? Definitely. But something else was different. He looked older. *Duh?!?* He was older. But he looked way older than he had last summer.

I wondered if they'd sent him to juvie hall for what he'd done last year on the last day of camp. Maybe being a counselor was part of his rehabilitation process, because he certainly needed rehabilitating. Still, I couldn't believe after the way he'd sabotaged our games that they would trust him —

"Jessica Kane," the woman on the porch said.

I snapped my attention to her. She was reading from a clipboard. What had she been saying before she announced my name? Was she taking roll call?

"Here!" I called out, raising my hand, standing on my toes so I could be more easily seen. Lacking in height had its drawbacks. And I was seriously vertically challenged. Not that I was a midget or a dwarf, but I had definitely inherited my mom's height, and she barely topped five feet.

Sean jerked his head around. Our gazes clashed, and I felt that little thrill of recognition that I'd experienced the first time we met—

"Put your hand down," Liz whispered harshly beside me.

"And Sean Reed," Amazon woman announced.

He snapped his head back to her, then twisted around completely to look at me. He took a defensive stance, crossing his arms over his chest. Something funny registered in his expression. A look of incredible disbelief. As though he'd been hit with a Taser gun. And then his mouth slowly turned up into that killer smile for which he was so well known.

A smile that before I got to know him always made my heart beat a little faster. Just like it was doing now. Old habits were hard to break. But I was so over Sean. Not that we'd ever been an item, but there had been a time when he'd drawn my interest. A time way before I really knew him, before I discovered he had the maturity level of a five-year-old.

"Why doesn't he answer roll call?" I asked.

"She's not taking roll, dummy," Liz said. "She's partnering people up. Weren't you listening?"

Apparently not.

"So whose name did she call out before she called mine? Who's my partner?"

"Geez, Jess, where were you?" Liz asked. "You're team member one. Team member two is . . . ta da! Sean."

"Sean Reed?"

"Do you see any other Sean around here?"

"That is so not going to work," I said. Now I completely understood the look that had crossed Sean's face. I figured my expression was looking exactly the same. It said, "No way, no way, no way. Absolutely not! That was so not going to happen."

Our matchup would be worse than the counselors' shorts and shirts. At least I could do a little creative altering with those. Sean had been unchangeable for four years. Always goofing around, playing practical jokes, never serious. Totally irritating. A royal pain in my—

Clang! Clang! Clang!

Again with the clanging of the iron triangle.

"All right, everyone, find your partners and form a circle," the woman said.

Liz started to walk off. I grabbed her arm. "Wait a minute. I'm totally lost. What *is* going on?"

She jerked her thumb toward the porch. "That's Edna and Ed. Apparently, they're the new people 'in charge' this year and are the ones who are going to train us. They're twins, by the way."

"They don't look anything alike." Although

really, what did I care about their relationship? They were setting me up for disaster.

"Whatever," Liz said. "Torie whispered to me that she'd heard they were twins. Anyway, they've paired everyone up—"

"I don't like the pairing."

She was looking seriously irritated with me. "I can't believe all this went totally over your head. This is lesson one. Learning to get along with whomever—"

"So *what*? They picked the worst possible matches they could come up with?" I couldn't help it, but I was starting to get a little freaked out!

"Couldn't have said it better myself," Sean said. "We have absolutely nothing in common."

I hadn't seen him approach. I wished that he hadn't. I could feel myself blushing. What could I say? We did have nothing in common. Last year proved that without question.

"Is there a problem over there?" Amazon Edna called out.

"I've gotta go," Liz said. Typical Liz, worried

about getting into trouble. Shouldn't a leader lead? Like lead a revolt against this insane pairing?

Liz walked away, leaving me facing Sean. His hair was cut shorter on the sides, but since he was wearing the CLS cap, I couldn't tell much about the top. Last year, he'd worn it spiked. It had made him look tough. And I'd sorta fallen for that tough-guy look. It had also made him look like a loner, but he'd spent a lot of time hanging around with a younger kid named Billy. I'd learned later that Billy was his brother. They looked nothing alike.

Now Sean shook his head. "I can't believe they paired me up with Paris Hilton."

I glowered. "I can't believe they paired me up with a cheater."

He shrugged like I'd said his worst offense was parting his hair on the wrong side.

"You weren't going to win anyway, so what difference did it make?" he asked.

I glared at him. It had been the final day of camp. The game had been Capture the Flag. Two teams competed for the prize: a plaque with the name of each member of the winning team inscribed on it. The plaque was given a place of honor on the wall inside the main office. My name was inscribed on three plaques.

Last year I had been the captain of Team One. Sean had been the captain of Team Two. Each team had been given compass directions to help us locate our base camp where our own flag flew. Once we reached our flag, we would find a map hidden beneath a nearby rock that gave us directions to the location of the other team's flag. The object, of course, was to find their flag, take it, and return it to our base camp—without being caught. Only Sean had somehow managed to replace our map with one that gave us a bogus location for his team's flag. Totally unfair!

"It makes a difference, Sean," I said, knowing it was pointless to even say it.

"Whatever."

His attitude angered me. His actions had put an end to my team's three-year winning streak. Maybe I could have accepted the defeat graciously if it had come about because the other team was better. Okay, probably not graciously. I had this thing about winning. I really, really liked to win. But I could have accepted the defeat grudgingly.

However, to lose because someone had cheated? How could he even think I would be okay with *that*? How could he not see that what he'd done had made him untrustworthy? I mean, who did he think he was?

And this first exercise was supposed to be about learning to get along? *I don't think so!*

To get along with a person you had to trust him or her. *Trust* and *Sean* were two words that did not go together—at least not in my dictionary.

Maybe the PTB (Powers That Be) at Camp Lone Star had forgiven him. But I never would.

Another clanging of the iron set my teeth further on edge.

"All right, everyone! Form your circle with partner one facing into the circle and partner two standing behind them," Edna said, sounding like a strange version of *The Cat in the Hat* with Thing One and Thing Two.

Put my back to Sean so he could stab me in it? Had she totally lost it?

"Come on!" Edna yelled.

Apparently, she had. What choice did I have? I didn't want to cause a scene and hadn't I answered yes to question eight? *Do you respect authority?*

Like everyone else, I shuffled around until I was standing in front of . . . my arch-nemesis. The Joker to my Batman. No way would I refer to him as my partner. I looked around the circle. Every partner one was a girl. Every partner two was a guy. Had the camp gone sexist?

"This week is all about trust," Edna announced. "Learning to trust yourselves. Learning to trust each other. Girls, I want you to close your eyes and fall backward. I want you to trust your partner to catch you."

Trust Sean? How?

"On the count of three," Edna said. "One, two, three!"

I spun around and stared at Sean. His blue eyes widened. His arms were actually outspread as though he'd planned to catch me. *Yeah, right, Jess. And if you enter* American Idol, *you'll be the next national sensation.*

"I'd rather fall facedown in mud than fall into your arms," I said.

"Fine," Sean ground out. "Play it that way."

Huh? Before I could react, Sean turned and fell backward.

I shrieked and staggered as his body knocked against mine. Of their own volition, my arms wrapped around his chest, holding him tightly against me.

I stood there stunned, doing what I thought I'd never do: Clutching Sean Reed as though my life depended on holding him as closely as possible.

Chapter Four XOXOX

Do you consider yourself mature?

Question fifteen on the counselor application. I had, of course, shaded in the yes oval with enthusiasm. My response was now questionable. A mature person didn't release her hold on a guy who had trusted her to catch him.

I'd let him go to prove a point. But when he'd landed on the ground with a hard thud, I wasn't exactly sure what my point had been, except maybe to demonstrate that I wasn't going to let him manipulate me this year. I wasn't going to fall for him, much less fall into his arms.

And Sean . . . what had Sean done after my demonstration of independence?

He'd just laughed, gotten up, made a big production of rubbing his backside, and announced, "Guess I was just too heavy for my partner."

Then he'd actually had the audacity to squeeze my upper arm. "We're going to have to work on building up your muscles. Miz Edna, is that part of the program this week? Getting stronger?"

He'd spoken loudly enough that everyone had heard. His comments had resulted in chuckles and snickers. I knew my face had turned red, because suddenly I was uncomfortably hot, embarrassed, and wondering when Sneaky Sean had become a Vince Vaughn wannabe.

Miz Edna seemed totally unconcerned that our little two-person team hadn't followed the exact directions regarding who was supposed to fall into whose arms. She simply said, "Everyone will definitely be stronger before the week is out."

Then she had tapped her clipboard. "Lunch is ready. We'll meet back out here in an hour to continue with leadership training."

So now I was sitting in the dining hall at a table with Liz, Caryn, and Torie. The partnering didn't extend to lunch, so girls were at one table, guys at another. For the moment, I could not have been happier with that arrangement. Having Sean at my table would have seriously ruined my appetite. As it was, I was struggling to eat anyway. My stomach was knotted tightly. I couldn't believe they'd hired him to be a counselor. What were they thinking? And how was I going to survive this?

"Falling into a guy's arms is so the way to start summer camp," Torie said. Last summer her hair had been blond. This summer it was black. Really black. Pulled back tightly into a ponytail. "You know what I'm saying?"

"Uh, actually, no, I don't," I said. I tried to sound like I was joking, but it came out sounding snippy.

"Yikes, girl," Caryn said. She was tall and slender with golden brown hair and eyes the same brown shade as her hair. "Be cool. Just because you couldn't trust your partner—"

"Would you have trusted Sean?" I interrupted.

She shrugged. "Maybe. He seems different this summer."

"In what way?"

"I don't know. We talked for a bit when we first got here. He seemed"—she shrugged again—"nicer than I remembered."

"Still, we can't overlook what he did at the end of last summer," Liz said. She was a true friend, completely understanding where I was coming from. "I mean, how can you trust someone who would blatantly cheat and then admit it?"

"I don't know," Torie said. "I think there's something admirable about admitting in front of everyone that you did something you shouldn't have. You know what I'm saying?"

I'd forgotten that Torie had the habit of ending every comment with, "You know what I'm saying?"

"No, I don't," I said. I also hadn't remembered that most of my responses to Torie's questions were the same thing. We were so out of sync. "Admitting you did something wrong doesn't change the fact that you did something wrong. It doesn't make it right."

"So ask for another partner," Caryn said.

I looked at the four other girl counselors who were sitting at the far end of our table. Eight girl counselors. Eight guy counselors. Would any of the girls be willing to trade? I didn't think so. Not when it meant trading down. As I'd overheard my mom tell Aunt Linda when she divorced husband number two to marry husband number three, you're supposed to trade up. (Mom didn't like her sister's husband number three nearly as much as she'd liked her husband number two.)

"It's only a week," Liz said. "It's not like you'll be partnered for the whole summer. I say just suck it up and endure. After all, summer camp is about roughing it. Sean will be a true test of your survival skills."

So much for Liz giving me total support. I wanted her to be PO'd, not meekly accept my situation. A leader was supposed to have strength of conviction. Plus, having to work with Sean was going to put a major damper on my flirtation opportunities.

"Easy enough for you to say. I noticed that you weren't in any hurry to separate yourself from your partner."

She gave me a huge grin. "Trent Smith. He's totally terrific: tall, dark, handsome, *and* remarkably strong."

"I don't remember him from last summer," I said, absently moving what looked to be orange worms, but was supposedly macaroni and cheese, around on my plate. Camp food was not exactly gourmet fare. I always looked forward to the nights when we toasted marsh-mallows on a fire or made s'mores. Even hot dogs roasted over an open fire tasted like heaven compared with what was usually served.

"I heard Trent's family recently moved to the area. He was a counselor at a campground in Orlando."

"What campground? Disney World?" I asked.

"I don't think so. Orlando is more than simply Disney World, you know."

"I was kidding," I said. Geez, had everyone lost their sense of humor? "Although wearing a Mickey Mouse costume might be preferable to our camp counselor getup."

"No kidding," Torie said.

She failed to follow that statement with her usual. Probably because she knew that we all knew what she was saying.

When we were finished eating and had put our trays in the dishwashing area—was I ever grateful washing dishes wasn't my job—we headed outside. Amazon Edna and Long-haired Ed were already out there, holding clipboards and talking. Edna was scowling. When she saw me, she deepened her scowl. She crooked her finger and wiggled it.

I glanced around. Just as I feared, she was crooking it at me. This had bad news written all over it. I swallowed and walked over. I tried really hard to look confident, to not let her know that my knees had started shaking. My internal cheerleader was chanting, *You go, girl! Take charge!*

"Yes, ma'am," I said respectfully when I arrived. I'd learned early on that politeness was a shortcut to an adult's good side. Besides, I'd answered question four—*Do you respect your elders?*—in the affirmative.

"I like freethinkers," she said. "People who don't conform."

Her words were so unexpected, so filled with praise that I couldn't help but smile. Here was clear evidence that changing up the uniform had been the way to go. I couldn't wait to tell Liz—maybe now she'd stop doubting my ideas.

"But—" she continued.

Oh, here it comes, I thought. *The reason behind the deep scowl.*

"Counselors have to be able to follow orders. Mutiny can't be tolerated."

"But the uni—"

"You are partner one," she said, interrupting

me before I could explain how hideously unflattering the uniforms were this year. "Sean is designated partner two. You were supposed to fall back into his arms. Not the other way around."

To my disappointment we weren't discussing the uniform. Bummer. It was so much easier to explain.

"But I didn't trust him," I blurted. Surely she could understand that. How could you let yourself fall when experience had taught you that the net wouldn't be there when you landed?

She nodded sagely. "That was obvious, but the quickest road to trust comes by building a bridge of common experiences."

Amazon Edna had quickly morphed into Yoda. I was certain she was trying to make a point, but she was going about it in a convoluted circle.

"Tonight you and Sean will be on evening shift dishwasher detail," she said.

She's kidding, right? Here I was, on my first day of CIT training and I was already being

45

punished? This was so unlike me, I just stood there, gaping.

Before I could sputter a response, Edna walked off. I assumed she was on her way to break the good news to Sean.

I was left standing in front of Long-haired Ed. I considered suggesting that he tell his twin to chill, but question seventeen on the application—*Do you play well with others?*—was haunting me. I'd answered yes to that one, too. Of course, I hadn't planned on being asked to play well with Sean.

"So, you and Edna are twins," I said instead, trying to sound like I was really interested. Maybe if I could get on his good side, he'd convince Edna to lighten up.

He laughed really loudly. For such a skinny guy he had an authentic Santa Claus belly-laugh going. "Check out snopes.com, and you'll discover that's an urban legend," he said. He patted my shoulder. "Maybe you and your camp partner can figure out the truth."

He walked off. And I was left with the real-ization that this entire week was going to involve people trying to hook me up with Sean.

Maybe a better name for the camp would be Camp Final Destination. Because being here was quickly turning into my worst nightmare!

Chapter Five

If Edna broke the news about our dishwashing assigment to Sean, it wasn't obvious. As a matter of fact, he'd walked out of the dining hall after lunch, whistling like he didn't have a care in the world. Then Edna had blown her own whistle—which was so much better than the clanging of the iron triangle.

Back in the main hall, she'd quickly jumped into a lecture on trust and its importance in our jobs. Again with the trusting ourselves, trusting each other. When we became experts in that regard, we would have no difficulty at all getting the campers—and their parents who were paying for camp—to trust us. We needed that trust to be successful as counselors.

I wanted nothing more than to be successful, but being paired up with Sean was like being paired up in chemistry class with the one guy who didn't understand chemistry. No way was your project going to get an A.

"We seem to have some trust issues in our group," she announced, and everyone swiveled his or her head around to look at me. Even my best friend.

Great! Just great! Not exactly the kind of attention I wanted.

"So we're going to learn by building trust," Edna continued. "Slowly. Everyone, find your designated partner and stand in front of him or her, facing each other."

It was with a great deal of undisguised reluctance that I trudged toward Sean, who trudged toward me. Only I was probably scowling, while he was smiling. He could only be in a good mood because he hadn't crossed paths with Edna yet and was still ignorant of our punishment for not playing by the rules.

"What are you grinning at?" I snapped.

His eyes widened. He glanced over one shoulder, then the other. He looked back at me and pressed both hands to his chest. "Are you talking to me?"

I rolled my eyes. "Forget it."

The piercing whistle sound echoed between the trees surrounding the camp. I looked at Edna. She was holding a stopwatch in her raised hand. "All right, CITs. I want you to stare into each other's eyes until I tell you to stop. Go!"

I jerked my attention back to Sean. "She can't be serious." I started to feel very nervous. Was I going to fail every exercise? But it was either that, or stare Sean in the eyes. I don't know why, but that scared me more.

"Based on the fact that we're washing dishes tonight, I think we can safely assume she has no concept of joking."

"She told you about our punishment?"

"Yep. Stop staring at my nose. I don't want to have to wash dishes tomorrow night, too."

I took a deep breath. *Chill,* I told myself. *This isn't a big deal.*

Then, I slowly, reluctantly, lifted my gaze to his. He had such blue eyes. A deeper, richer blue than my own. How could someone with such beautiful eyes be such a jerk?

"Why do you think she's making us do this?" I asked.

"The dishes?"

"No. The staring."

"I don't know. It's got something to do with trust. That seems to be one of her favorite words."

"So I noticed. Maybe she's the one with trust issues."

"Could be."

"Ed says they're not twins."

I wasn't sure why I was yammering except that it kept me distracted, prevented me from really noticing the depths of his eyes. *Eyes are windows to the soul,* my grandma had always said. I really didn't want to look into Sean's soul.

"Why would they be twins?" Sean asked.

"That's what Torie said."

"Yep, and there are bears in the woods," he said sarcastically.

Before I could respond to that tacky reminder of last summer's makeover interruption, Edna finally yelled, "Time!"

I let out a deep breath and turned my attention to Edna. I'd gotten off easy. Fifteen seconds tops, staring into those eyes. Eyes that made me wish I could trust him, made me wish I liked him, because honestly they were nice to look into. . . .

"Did you feel the connection?" Edna asked. "Gazing into someone's eyes forces you to truly notice him — or her. Take a step toward your partner."

"Define step," I mumbled, wondering if easing forward the length of my big toe could count as a step.

Apparently, Sean interpreted *step* to mean the length of his foot. And he had large feet. He was suddenly a lot closer to me, the toes of his hiking boots practically touching mine. I wanted to take a giant step back, but his eyes held a dare, like he was challenging me, knew he was encroaching on my personal space, and if I stepped back, he'd win.

I can't explain how I knew all those thoughts were going through his head. But I did. And I wasn't one to back down. Call me stubborn, but there you have it. I stood my ground.

"All right," Edna called out. "Take each other's hands."

Sean wiped his hands on his shorts like maybe he was nervous and like he seriously thought I was going to follow Edna's order. Maybe he thought I was going to do as instructed because I was rubbing my sweating palms on my shorts, too. Not that I was going to hold his hands, but it gave me something to do, as I tried to figure out how to get myself out of this situation. Usually I was good at strategy. It was the reason my name was etched on three plaques hanging in the main lodge, along with those of my team members from the past three end-of-summer Capture the Flag games.

"Anyone not holding hands will spend time

in the jail," Edna announced like some drill sergeant.

I should explain that the "jail" is this little shed with bars on the windows. I think it might have once been an outhouse. It's really small and all dilapidated-looking. And it smells funny. The door doesn't even close properly. It hangs at an odd angle, so it's not like anyone can seriously be locked inside. It's more of an embarrassment thing.

I'd never spent time there, but Sean had. Last summer he and some guys had been the ones cutting up and causing our canoe to turn over, spilling all of us into the lake.

"Been there, done that," Sean said grumpily, grabbing my hands before I could protest.

Something, almost like an electric shock, traveled through me. Holding Sean's hands was nothing at all like taking hold of my brother's hand and leading him through the Six Flags theme park toward the roller coaster.

"I've never done it," I said, trying to wrench free. But he was holding on too tightly.

"Trust me. You don't want to."

Trust him? How could he even utter those two words to me after what he'd done?

I was going to pull really hard, but I noticed people were beginning to look around. Probably wondering why Edna was standing still with her hands on her hips and a disgruntled look on her face. She was getting PO'd. If I wasn't careful, I really might not pass CIT training. And that would be horrible. I wasn't in the habit of not achieving my goals. That was part of the reason I was still so mad at Sean about last summer. He'd thwarted me. For some reason, I just couldn't find it in me to forgive him again.

But with a sigh, I accepted that Liz was right. It was only seven days. I could endure his close proximity for that long.

I just hoped there wasn't going to be a lot of touching going on, because his touch really unsettled me. I stopped struggling and nodded at Edna. She nodded back. Ed smiled. What was that about?

"All right," Edna shouted. "Stare into your partner's eyes again. . . . Now!"

"Not my chin," Sean said.

"Why not? I got lucky before."

"Yeah, but when your luck runs out, I get punished."

I was looking back into his eyes. "For what it's worth, I thought Edna overreacted to our situation this morning."

"Most definitely," he said.

We were quiet for a couple of seconds. I was amazed at how loud quiet could sound. And how much I liked looking into Sean's eyes. And holding his hands. I needed a distraction.

"This is totally weird," I finally said.

"I don't know. I kinda like it. You've got really pretty blue eyes."

Not as pretty as yours . . . but I wasn't about to say that! "A compliment?" I asked instead.

"We could trade compliments if you want, while we're standing here doing nothing."

"We're not doing *nothing*. We're staring. That's *something*."

"You're trying to change the subject. We were discussing compliments. I give you one. You give me one. That's how it works."

"No way. That's not how it works. Compliments don't mean trade-offs."

"You sure?"

"Definitely." Besides, what kind of compliment could I really give him? Although being this close to him, staring into his eyes, seeing his face in my peripheral vision, I was beginning to realize what had changed about him. He didn't look nearly as young as he had last summer. He looked not just a year older but a lot older. A little more rugged, even.

Were more than his looks different? *Was* he the kind of guy that a girl could now trust? Could fall for? And if he was, was I in danger of falling for him?

"Time!" Edna yelled.

Thank goodness! My thoughts had started traveling a path they had no business being on.

Sean let go of my hands as though they'd suddenly ignited. I wondered if the same unsettling thoughts had been going through his mind.

I immediately stepped back and lowered my gaze. It seemed to me that an excellent exercise at this point in time would be trading partners. Shouldn't we be switching around constantly so we learned to deal with all types of people, not just one person?

Maybe I should discuss that strategy with Edna. I mean, this was her first year at the camp—she was new. She might appreciate some helpful advice. Besides, it would allow me to prove that I'd answered question seven—*Do you like to help others?*—truthfully.

Edna gave us a little more advice about looking a person in the eye when we talked to him. Touching someone. Offering comfort. Connecting. It was all about connecting and easing into another person's personal space without invading it—like welcoming someone into your house. Then she told us to get settled in, and we'd start seriously learning in the morning.

Gosh, if all this hadn't been serious stuff, I wasn't certain that I wanted tomorrow to come. What was next? Hugging your partner? Still, I couldn't get away from Sean fast enough.

Liz, unfortunately, seemed in no hurry to

get away from Trent. They were still gazing into each other's eyes, and she had this really silly grin on her face. Come to think of it, he had a goofy grin, too.

"Ah, young love," Sean said in a low voice near my ear.

I jerked back and glared at him. "Like you'd know anything about love."

"I've heard rumors."

Was he trying to be funny?

I shook my head slightly. That was so not what I'd expected him to say. I was sure he'd think he was a love god or something. I really didn't know Sean at all. Which was fine. Because I really didn't want to know him.

"What about you, Jessica?" he said, stunning me by actually using my real name. "Do you have a boyfriend?"

"I am so not discussing my love life with you."

"Is that because you don't have one to discuss?"

His stupid question didn't even deserve an

answer. I turned on my heel and headed toward the dormitory.

It was none of his business that I did not, in fact, have a love life. That I'd never had a love life. Or that I'd never even been kissed. Hadn't even come close.

Chapter Six

XOXOX

As it turned out, Liz, Torie, Caryn, and I were sharing the dormitory. Torie and Caryn had arrived earlier and had been out scouting the area. That's the reason we hadn't met up until the first meeting of the morning.

I was excited that we would all be sharing space, because we'd gotten along great last year. It was reassuring that at least one aspect of the camp was going right! As I got settled in, I tried really hard not to think about everything that had gone wrong so far.

On the wall above my bed I hung a dream catcher that I'd made last summer. According to Lakota legend, the web captures the good parts of dreams, while the bad parts slip through the hole in the center. I wasn't sure that I really believed in the power of the legend, but I liked the story. And I definitely needed something to hold on to the good. To ward off the evil of Sean.

At the foot of my bed, I placed an afghan that my grandma had crocheted for me when I started kindergarten, so I would have something to snuggle against during nap time. I didn't take naps anymore, but I liked to wrap up in it whenever I read. It reminded me of snuggling against my grandma. Not that we had a lot of spare time at camp, but I was hoping to finish rereading my Harry Potter books before the final one came out. I was halfway finished with *Harry Potter and the Goblet of Fire*. Two summers ago, I'd made the beaded bookmark that I used to mark my place.

On the nightstand beside my bed, I put a

picture of my family—Mom, Dad, Alex, and me—all bundled up. A ski slope was in the background. We'd gone to Telluride, Colorado, during the holidays. I also had a photo of Liz and me, hamming it up the last day of school. We were grinning, giving each other a big thumbs-up. We had made it. We were on our way to high school.

If we could get through the summer.

By the time Liz, Caryn, Torie, and I had everything in place, Ed was clanging the triangle to signal that supper was ready. I wasn't thrilled that the afternoon had drifted away. Nor was I exactly thrilled with the supper menu. Not only were there separate plates for the corn bread and chocolate cake but bowls for the stew. Way too many dishes to wash.

Just like lunch, the tables were divided by gender. A table of girls, a table of boys.

"So did we not get the cutest guys as partners?" Torie asked after we all sat down at our table.

"We did not," I said.

"Oh, come on," Caryn said. "You might not like Sean, but you have to admit that he is cute."

I didn't have to admit anything.

"I wouldn't have minded staring into his eyes for a couple of minutes," Liz said.

Traitor.

"Did you want to switch partners?" I asked.

"No way. But I agree with Caryn that Sean is cute."

"I think he's a perfect example of not judging a book by its cover," I said.

"The guys are staring at us," Caryn whispered, ducking her head down slightly, staring into her bowl of stew. "Do you think they're as interested in us as we are in them?"

"I'm not interested," I said.

"Come on, Jess, you might not be interested in Sean, but there are plenty of other guys. So who do you wish you'd been partnered with?" Liz asked.

Hmmm. Good question.

Very subtly, I slid my gaze over so I could

examine the guys at the first table. I was surprised to see Sean looking at me. Or at least I thought he was. It was like our eyes met for a split second. Then, like Caryn, he was suddenly very interested in his stew. Maybe he was wondering how much work it would be to wash all these dishes.

Some of the other guys at the table were definitely cute, especially the guy in a green shirt, sitting near the end of the table. I didn't know him. But my gaze kept wandering back to Sean. *Obnoxious Sean. Cheating Sean.* I needed the refrain to keep cycling through my head so I wouldn't forget.

"If I was only about looks, I'd have to admit that Sean would definitely be boyfriend material," I said, somewhat reluctantly. Then I realized something else. Sean was wearing a black T-shirt that fit him way better than his camp shirt. "Why are the guys not in their uniforms?"

"Excellent question," Liz said.

Everyone at our table was suddenly seriously looking around. We were the only ones still dressed in brown.

Liz leaned over to the girls at the far end of our table. "Why aren't you still in uniform?"

"Pul-ease!" the girl said. She was blond. I think her name was Kimo.

"Don't we have to wear them?" Liz asked.

"Only when we're officially 'on duty.'" She tapped her bowl. "We're not on duty."

"Oh, cool. We must have missed that announcement." Liz straightened and grinned at us. "I say we head back to the dormitory as soon as we're finished eating and change."

"Can't," I said.

"Why not?" Liz asked.

I grimaced. I'd somehow thought that not discussing my kitchen duty might make it go away, but the way Edna kept looking at me from her place at the head table, I knew I was doomed.

"I have to wash the dishes tonight." I looked down at my plate.

Liz gasped as though I'd just told her that she could no longer be my best friend.

"What are you talking about?"

I repeated my earlier conversation with Edna word for word. It was emblazoned on my brain, forever burning its way into my most undesirable memories.

"That's so not fair!" Liz announced.

Although I agreed with her, I was trying really hard not to prove that I'd answered question ten on the application wrong: *Do you have a positive outlook? Yes.*

I shrugged. "Could be worse. She could have us cleaning the toilets."

Although a half hour later when I was standing in the kitchen with Sean, I was thinking that maybe cleaning toilets wouldn't be so bad.

Jackson was the guy in charge of the kitchen. I didn't know if that was his first name or his last. He didn't have anything embroidered on his apron. He was a pretty large man—maybe he believed in sampling the food as he cooked it. He had a small staff of three people who helped him cook and clean. They were thrilled—

doing the happy dance around the kitchen—because tonight, at least, they didn't have to wash dishes.

Needless to say, I was less than thrilled. But apparently Sean was digging it.

He stood beside me in front of the side-by-side stainless-steel sinks. Each had a long-hosed nozzle. We simply rinsed off the plates or bowls, watched the food circle the drain and go down the disposal, and placed the dishes in the large dishwasher beside us. Each machine was about three times bigger than the one in my kitchen at home. I guess they needed extra dishwashing power to handle all the dishes they had to deal with once camp got underway. I'd never really given it any thought. Just assumed some dishwashing fairy came in every night and took care of things. *Silly me.*

Sean was humming a song and squirting the plates in rhythm to his humming. *Da-squirt-da-squirt-dada-squirt-squirt.*

"How can you be so jovial?" I asked.

"How can you not?" he retorted.

"I don't even wash dishes at home."

"I do," he said. "So, what am I humming?"

Da-squirt-da-squirt-dada-squirt-squirt.

"The theme song to *Mission Impossible.*"

"Wrong!"

I stared at him. "No way."

"*Mission Impossible Three.*"

"Like there's a difference."

"Of course there's a difference. If there wasn't, it would simply be *Mission Impossible.*"

Da-squirt-da-squirt-dada-squirt-squirt.

Then he changed songs.

Hum-squirt-hum-squirt-hum-huh-hum-uh-squirt-squirt.

He bent down slightly and knocked his shoulder against mine. That was another thing that was different about him. He was a lot taller this summer, which left me feeling a lot shorter.

"Come on, Travel Size. Take a guess," he urged.

I raised my eyebrows at him. "Excuse me? 'Travel Size'?"

"Yeah, you don't really seem to be growing in between summers."

"I'll have you know that girls reach their

full height way ahead of guys. I just reached mine sooner than most."

"You don't have to be so sensitive about it. I dig shortness in chicks."

I shook my head in disbelief. *Like I care what he digs in chicks.*

"I'm not sensitive about my height. I'm sensitive that you seem to think you have the right to give me nicknames."

"I give everyone nicknames. It's what I do."

"That and get into trouble," I reminded him.

"I get into trouble when I'm bored. Washing dishes is boring. We're CITs. We're supposed to know how to make things fun."

Question thirteen. Are you able to make the most boring of tasks exciting?

And, of course, I'd answered yes.

"So come on," he continued. "Guess the movie."

Hum-squirt-hum-squirt-hum-huh-hum-uh-squirt-squirt.

"*Star Wars,*" I finally said.

"Which episode or title?"

"They're all the same."

"No, they're not. I'm thinking of a particular episode."

"*Episode Three: Revenge of the Sith.*"

"Nope. *Episode Four: A New Hope.*"

I rolled my eyes. "And if I'd said Episode Four, you would have said Episode Three."

"You've got major trust issues," Sean said.

"With you, definitely."

"Come on. It's been a year. People change."

"People, sure. But Freddy Krueger? I don't think so."

"Ouch! I'm not that bad."

"The snake in my bed?" I reminded him.

He grimaced. "That was four years ago. And it was a harmless garden snake."

It hadn't looked harmless slithering across my sheet when I'd pulled back the covers before getting into bed. Needless to say my scream had been heard throughout the camp.

"The face painting? A scorpion?" I continued.

It was a rainy day, and the counselors had decided to keep us occupied by letting us paint something on each other's cheeks.

"You wanted a butterfly. That's so girly-girl."

"I *am* a girl. Girly-girl is what I do."

"Right. Just like Paris Hilton." He glanced over at me. "This is camp! You know? The outdoors, the woods, back to nature. And you're dressing up like you're going to the prom!"

I knew he was back to discussing the makeover night. Why did it bug him so much?

"Well, we were having a girls' night! No one was supposed to see us."

He grinned. "Well, we were having a guys' night."

"And your idea of fun was scaring us?"

He chuckled. "Pretty lame, I know, but you looked so funny running out of the cabin—"

"I don't get why you found that hilarious."

"Come on, it was a practical joke. You took it way too seriously. As for the scorpion I painted on your cheek . . . you have to admit, it was way cool."

I didn't have to admit anything. At least not out loud. But inside my head, where he couldn't hear, I did admit that the scorpion was way cool, shades of black, dark blue, and green.

Sean was an awesome artist—the reason I'd agreed to let him paint something on my cheek to begin with.

I guess he got tired of waiting for me to respond because he said, "Okay. One more."

"One more what?"

Da-squirt-da-squirt-da-da—

"*Jaws,*" I said. "One, two, three, and into infinity."

"We have a winner!" he shouted.

Then he squirted cold water into my face!

Chapter Seven

I shrieked, crouched, and retaliated!

I sprayed him like a painter with a spray gun trying to quickly paint the outside of a house. I swept my arm up, down, around.

He was yelling, laughing, hunkering down. Our weapons, attached to the faucet, severely limited our mobility and ability to escape or duck for cover. We were mostly aiming for the face. My hair was drenched. Water was running down my forehead. It occurred to me that it was a good thing my mom wasn't into letting me wear makeup yet or it would have been all over my face, and Sean would have had one more thing to laugh about.

As it was, his laughter was echoing around us. He seemed to be having such a great time. I didn't want to admit that I was, too. Especially since I was getting him good and wet.

"Hey! What's going on in here?" a loud masculine voice yelled.

We both turned, and Jackson took a direct hit. That stopped the water war. Cold.

Jackson was not a happy camper. He planted his beefy hands on his hips.

"My bad," Sean said.

What was this? He was going to take the blame? What game was he playing now? If he was trying to get on my good side, lying wasn't the way to get there.

"Actually we're both to blame," I said.

"I started it," he said.

I'd just opened my mouth to respond when Jackson barked, "I don't care who started it. I only care that it got ended. Mops are in the closet there." He pointed one of his sausage-shaped fingers at a door. "Get this mess cleaned up."

"Yes, sir," Sean and I said at the same time. For once, we were in complete accord.

Jackson stormed out of the area, and I could hear him barking orders at the other workers. I released the breath I hadn't realized I'd been holding. I shifted my gaze over to Sean. "You're a trouble magnet, you know that?"

"Hey, I was willing to take the blame."

"Being a CIT means not shirking responsibility."

"I started it."

I couldn't help myself. I smiled at him. His black hair—no longer spiked, but longer in the front—was plastered to his head, his dren-ched T-shirt plastered to his body. "But I finished it."

He gave me one of his famous devilish grins. "No way! Jackson finished it."

"I was close to finishing it, though."

His grin broadened. "Yeah, you were." He reached out and tugged on several strands of my wet hair. "I can't see Paris Hilton getting down and dirty."

My heart was suddenly thundering. What was happening here? Were we flirting with each other? Was I actually enjoying his attention?

Self-conscious, I stepped back, which resulted in his yanking on my hair. I swiped at his hand. "Let go."

He dropped his hand to the side. I was glad he wasn't touching me anymore. Wasn't I? Most definitely.

"We need to get this mess cleaned up," I said unnecessarily. Anything to distract me, him—us—from what had been happening for those few weird seconds.

"Right," he said.

It didn't take us that long. The kitchen area was actually set up for fast cleanup. I suppose most nights they just sprayed the cement floor down.

Still, it was almost dark when we left the dining hall and started walking back to our dormitory. Later in the summer, the sun would stay out longer. But for now, the peacefulness of the night settled in earlier; I could hear the crickets and the frogs.

A lake was nearby. I'd loved swimming in it, being on it last summer. Unfortunately, the water was really cold at the beginning of summer, so I knew it would be a while before we could go swimming.

"Can I be honest with you?" Sean suddenly asked.

I rolled my eyes. "That would be a departure for you, wouldn't it? Being honest?"

"Cut me some slack, would you? I helped you clean up the mess you made in the kitchen, didn't I?"

I stopped walking and stared at him. "I made the mess? Fifteen minutes ago you admitted to starting it."

"Yeah, but if you'd simply taken it like a good little girl—"

"No way was I going to just *take* getting sprayed."

"All right. You have a point. I was the instigator. Anyway, back to being honest . . ."

I waited, wondering if he was going to comment on our strange flirtation in the kitchen. Was he going to admit to feeling *something*? I don't know what. Something like a tug on his heart? Was he going to admit—

"You didn't really win."

I stared at him. "What?"

"The song I was humming. You sorta cheated, by naming all the *Jaws* movies."

"I cheated?" I couldn't read his expression.

He started backing away from me. "I don't know if I can trust you now."

"Sean—"

"I'm pretty sure I can't," he said.

"This is stupid. You can trust me."

He moved his hands back and forth between us like the robot in *I, Robot.* "Trust works both ways."

Now I realized: He was making fun of me!

"No way will I trust you. Ever!"

"We'll see."

And with that, he turned and ran to the guys' dormitory.

I wanted to yell something at him, but I was

beginning to sound like my dad's TiVo when something happened to its disk and it kept replaying the same two seconds of a show.

I definitely needed to talk to Edna about getting a new partner.

Chapter Eight

L ater that night, after lights-out, I was lying on my bed staring into the darkness. I kept hearing Sean's annoying humming in my head. It gets really, really dark in the woods. Living in the city, before I started coming to summer camp, I never realized how much of the darkness is really light—light from the streetlights, the traffic lights, and nearby stores. But out here in the wilderness, it's totally dark.

And quiet. No cars rushing past. No honks. No sirens.

There's a peacefulness. A calmness. An

eeriness. It's not scary. It's just very, very different.

I heard a noise off to my right. The creak of a bed. Bare feet slapping on the floor.

"Jess?" Liz whispered. "Are you ready?"

"For what?"

"Oh, gosh, I forgot to tell you. We're meeting up with some other CITs down by the lake."

I sat up. "When did you decide to do this?"

"When you had kitchen duty. Then you came in all wet, and by the time you finished explaining *that* story . . ."

Her voice trailed off. Without me there, I wondered who'd talked Liz into doing something we weren't supposed to be doing. But someone had, because she was totally up for it, no doubt in her voice at all. Then I felt a pang—it wasn't often that Liz made plans without me. But I pushed the feeling away.

I tossed back the sheet. I was ready for an adventure. I threw on some jeans and a long-sleeved T-shirt.

We all dug our flashlights out of our footlockers. That was one piece of equipment we were required to bring. That and lots of batteries. Did I mention the camp has no stores?

I mean the staff has supplies delivered daily so we aren't in danger of starving or anything. Plus a small town is nearby in case we get into any kind of real trouble or need help in an emergency. But other than that, not much out here resembles civilization.

Now, Liz, Caryn, Torie, and I were shuffling toward the door without turning on our flashlights, going slowly so we didn't make any noise. Edna and Ed were probably already in bed. Asleep. They looked like the early-to-bed, early-to-rise types. But why take a chance on disturbing them?

Our late-night mischief was incredibly exciting. As a camper, we'd never been able to sneak out at night because our counselors had always been light sleepers. Not that we would have been that adventurous. But this summer was different.

This summer we were all about adventure, being bold, taking risks.

We crept to the door.

"Look outside," Liz ordered in a whisper.

"Who are you talking to?" I asked.

"You."

I was quickly discovering that CITs all had one thing in common: Each wanted to be the boss. Each thought her way was the best way.

"Who made you boss?" Caryn asked.

"We don't have time for this," Torie said. "The guys are waiting. You know what I'm saying?"

"No, I don't. What guys?" I asked.

I really felt like I was in the dark—figuratively as well as literally.

"The guys we're meeting," Caryn said.

"You said we were meeting the other CITs."

"And the other CITs are guys."

"Not all of them."

"All the ones we're meeting are."

Suddenly, I had an uneasy feeling. "Are we meeting up with our partners?"

As though tired of the inquisition, Caryn opened the door and peered out. I know it was her because the porch light washed over her face. The camp kept porch lights on all night. As a matter of fact, they were light sensitive: They turned on with the arrival of twilight; they turned off with the arrival of dawn. No one had to think about them.

"All clear," Caryn said.

Then the others were rushing out the door, giving me no choice except to follow. No way was I staying in the dormitory alone, while they were out flirting with some guys. Besides, maybe I could get close enough to another guy that we could convince Edna and Ed to swap out our partners.

I couldn't be the only person unhappy with the way that we'd all been paired up.

Because of the various porch lights on the different buildings we were able to make our way to the woods without any mishaps. Once we were hidden behind some trees, Liz turned on her flashlight. She released a tiny squeal and pointed to a low-hanging branch on a nearby tree.

A length of toilet paper was draped over it.

How totally romantic. Not!

She reached for it —

"We should probably leave it," Caryn said. "So we can find our way back."

"Right," Liz said. "First rule of survival: Leave bread crumbs."

"Yeah, like they ever do that on *Survivor*," Torie said.

"I wish we could vote a CIT out of leadership boot camp," I muttered as Liz headed for the next dangling bit of white.

"Maybe you should report that he sprayed water on you," she said.

So he could report that I fired back? Besides, the kitchen guy saw us. Geez, I hoped Jackson wasn't going to report us. It hadn't occurred to me that he might. After all, we cleaned up our mess. And we didn't argue about it. We just did it.

I shrugged, even though no one could see me since it was fairly dark, even with the flashlights — we'd all turned ours on now. "It was just water. It wasn't like he took the butcher knife after me."

"He may have been thinking it, though," Liz said.

"Liz!"

"What? I don't think he likes you any more than you like him."

"But he does trust her," Caryn said. "Otherwise he wouldn't have fallen into her arms like he did."

"You know, not only do I feel like we're walking in circles, but we're *talking* in circles. Haven't we covered this ground before?" I asked.

"You mean the path or the topic?" Torie asked.

"Both."

Everyone came to a stop.

"You don't think the guys are messing with us, do you?" Caryn asked. "I mean, are they like hanging around to jump out at us or something? To scare us, to make us scream? You know, like they did last summer?"

"Of course not," Liz said. "They're not kids anymore."

"Did you not see me when I came back from

kitchen duty?" I asked.

"That's different. That was Sean. Trent is so not like Sean."

"And you know that because you looked into his eyes for two minutes?"

"We connected." She turned around and pointed the light so it chased away the darkness—

And we all screamed because someone dark and mysterious was standing there!

Chapter Nine XOXOX

"Quiet!" the guy said, using the kind of voice you use when you're trying to be quiet but be heard at the same time.

"Oh, Trent," Liz said and laughed. "You scared us."

Three guys were behind him and I recognized one — Sean.

"We came looking for you because it was taking so long. Come on." He took her hand — took her hand! — and led her through the woods.

Caryn and Torie fell into step beside two

guys, which left me with Sean. *Traitors!*

I thought about turning around and heading back to the dormitory, but I didn't for two reasons:

1. I refused to let Sean dictate what I would or wouldn't do.

2. I didn't want to be alone and possibly miss out on some fun. Wandering through the woods at night could prove to be exciting. At least it would be different from the adventures we'd had during previous summers.

Suddenly, Sean stopped. "Hey, guys, sshh!"

Everyone stopped.

"What is it?" Trent whispered.

"Thought I heard something."

"A bear?" I asked sarcastically.

"No. There are no bears in these woods," Sean said. "Remember?"

I remember.

"What is it then?" Trent asked.

"Do you think Ed or Edna saw us leave our dormitory?" Sean asked.

I know my eyes got big and round—like full

moons. "*You're* worried about getting into trouble?"

"Yeah, relax, man," one of the other guys said. "The worst we'll get is some jail time."

He was referring to the camp jail, not actually being arrested by the sheriff's department or anything.

"Why don't we just do whatever we're going to do here?" Sean asked.

"What are we going to do?" I asked, suddenly suspicious.

"Works for me," Trent said. "But let's move off the trail."

"What are we going to do?" I whispered again as I followed everyone farther into the woods.

"Beats me," Sean said. "All these plans were made while I was cleaning up the kitchen."

"While *we* were cleaning the kitchen," I reminded him.

"And whose fault was it that we had to clean the kitchen?"

I refused to be baited again.

Everyone came to a stop.

"This'll work," Trent said.

It was then that I noticed the girls were spreading out blankets. I hadn't seen them carrying them before. We had serious miscommunication going on here.

"Hello? You didn't tell me to bring a blanket."

"Well, duh, you don't want to sit on the ground," Torie said. "You know what I'm saying?"

"That's her favorite phrase, isn't it?" Sean whispered.

I ignored him. I swept my flashlight over the ground until I spotted a log. That would work. As a rule, I'm okay with nature and sitting on the ground, but at night . . . I didn't want to think about what might be crawling around. And I had on a pretty new pair of jeans from the Gap.

Sean sat beside me.

"Find your own log," I said.

"This is my log," he said. "I carved my name on it earlier in the day."

"Really, dude? That's awesome," one of the guys said.

Torie introduced him. Jet. His name was Jet. Or so he claimed. I couldn't imagine a mom naming her kid Jet. But he was Torie's partner.

The other guy was Jon—no H. That was how he actually introduced himself. Jon—no H. He was Caryn's partner.

We'd all set our flashlights on the ground so it was like having an artificial fire going. Each girl was sitting beside her partner, and I was kinda wondering what the plans were.

"So why are we here?" I finally asked when the suspense got to be too much.

"We just wanted to get to know each other better," Trent said.

"It's no accident, dudes, that E & E matched the guys in one dormitory with the babes in another. It's dormitory A and B against C and D," Jet said. "We want an advantage, so we can win."

"What are we winning?" I asked.

"Respect, man."

"We just thought it would be nice to get to know each other better," Liz finally said. "No big deal. We'll all go to the same high school next year, right?"

"Memorial High," everyone murmured.

"You know what we need?" Caryn asked. "An icebreaker."

"Dude, there's ice out here?" Jet asked.

This guy was really a CIT?

"I think he's a battery short of having a working flashlight," Sean whispered close to my ear.

A shiver went through me. I told myself it wasn't because he was so near. It was simply the brush of his breath over my neck. Like the shiver that goes down your spine when someone supposedly walks over your future grave site.

Or it could have been his words causing the shiver. It was kinda scary, because I'd been thinking almost the same thing, although a little kinder maybe—that Jet was like a Will Ferrell character.

Torie laughed. "You're so goofy." She shoved

Jet's shoulder. "I know you're just teasing."

I wondered how she knew that, because he'd sounded totally serious to me.

"Anyway, when Edna had us fall into each other's arms this afternoon, that was an ice-breaker," Caryn explained.

"Thought it was a lesson in trust," Jon—no H—said.

"That, too. Anyway." Caryn shifted on to her hip, reached into her back pocket, and pulled out a piece of paper. "I'm really into dream interpretation. My dad's a psychiatrist so he's been teaching me what he knows. We could learn something about each other by sharing our dreams."

"No way am I sharing my dreams," Sean said.

The other guys were quick to agree with Sean. Guys never seem interested in revealing their innermost selves. I could have told Caryn the guys wouldn't go for it.

"You don't have to tell me the details. Just the major color," Caryn said.

"Dude, mine are black and white," Jet said.

"You're kidding," I said. "You dream in black and white?"

"Yeah, I figured everybody did."

We went around the circle. Jon and Jet were the only ones to dream in black and white. I wondered what that meant.

"So what does that say about us?" Jon asked.

Caryn looked seriously disappointed. "I don't know."

"What does it mean if you dream in color?" Liz asked.

"Depends on the color."

"Last night my dream was mostly red," Liz said.

"That's an easy one," Caryn said. "It means stop. Consider your actions."

"The actions in your dream?" I asked.

"No, your actions in real life. What happens in a dream reflects what's going on in your real world, but it disguises it so you can deal with it more easily."

"Why can't it mean you're angry?" Sean

asked. And I sorta wondered the same thing. Scary. Similar Sean thoughts. "Don't people say they see red when they're angry? So if you're dreaming red—"

"That's not what it means," Caryn insisted.

"Dream interpretation isn't an exact science, is it?" Sean asked.

"Okay," Caryn said, clearly exasperated. "You come up with an icebreaker."

"Sure." He grinned. "Truth or Dare?"

The guys jumped on that as though Sean had offered them free tickets to the Super Bowl. I figured they expected the dares to involve kisses or a team going into the woods alone—without the other teams.

I'd played the game with my girlfriends at a slumber party, but no way was I going to play it out here in the woods, in the dark, with three guys I didn't know and one I absolutely didn't trust.

"I'd rather have my dreams interpreted," I said. "They're mostly blue."

"Oh!" Caryn said eagerly as though she was

no more interested in a game of Truth or Dare than I was. She shined her flashlight on a scrap of paper that looked like it had come out of a magazine. There was a circle divided into colors. "That's easy. You see things clearly. Blue is the color of truth."

"And the color of dare?" Sean asked.

"We're not playing Truth or Dare," I said.

"Who put you in charge?"

I shot to my feet. "What are we doing here? If Ed and Edna find out what we're doing—"

"What are we doing, Jess?" Liz asked. "We're just sitting out here talking, trying to get to know each other better."

This was my friend Liz? The same Liz who, earlier in the day, had worried about changing the look of her uniform?

"It feels like we're doing something we shouldn't, something that could get us into serious trouble," I said.

"And you never do something you shouldn't?" Sean asked.

"You say that like behaving is a fault."

"It's Boresville."

Was that the reason I'd never had a boyfriend? Because I was dull, boring? Unexciting?

"I'm going back to the dormitory," I said.

"I'll go with you," Liz said.

"No, stay if you want. I can follow the ever-so-original toilet-paper trail."

"Okay. If you're sure," she said.

Liz had never not stuck by me. My comment had been just a bluff. I hadn't expected her to call me on it.

I walked back to camp, feeling totally alone.

It was really important to me to be the very best CIT that I could be. Like the marines. Be all that you can be.

We were supposed to learn to trust each other. To trust ourselves. How could I do that when my best friend had just abandoned me? For a guy she'd met just a few hours ago?

This was supposed to be the best summer ever. And it had gotten off to such a rotten start.

Had I really walked away from my best friend?

And where had my sense of adventure disappeared to?

What would they all be thinking about me now? What would Sean think? Oh, well. Since when did I care about what Sean thought?

Chapter Ten

XOXOX

The next morning, following a breakfast of rubbery pancakes and extra-pulp orange juice, all the CITs gathered in front of the main building. The ringing of the iron triangle was still reverberating through the chill of the morning. In another six weeks there would be no coolness at all. The humidity factor would skyrocket. But for now, things were still pleasant. Not too many bugs. That, too, would change.

Edna gave the order for us to partner up.

"Did this place morph into a dude ranch

while we were sleeping?" I muttered.

Liz laughed at my pitiful joke. She, Caryn, and Torie had returned to the dormitory last night about half an hour after I did. Apparently, no one had been able to agree on an icebreaker, and some of the noises they began to hear convinced them that maybe being out in the woods alone at night wasn't too smart. Even if no bears roamed the area.

Especially since we ended up going to sleep so late and had to get up so early.

I am so not a morning person. Not even at camp. I was wondering if I should rethink my summer plans. Especially when Sean arrived at my side, grinning.

Of course he'd be a morning person. I should have known. I looked down and straightened my stupid brown shirt. Today I'd worn it with the sleeves rolled up and only one button done, over a light green tank top. I wondered if Sean thought I looked silly. Probably.

"Still mad at me?" he asked.

"*Still* gives the impression there was a

moment in time when I wasn't mad at you," I said.

His grin broadened. Why didn't he look dorky in his uniform? "Come on. There has to be some time when you weren't mad at me?"

I shook my head. "Can't think of any."

"How 'bout last summer when I taught you how to feed the baby bird?"

During one of the weekly scavenger hunts, he'd found a bird with a broken wing. It hadn't been on the list of things to find that we'd been given, but nothing on the list had been as interesting. The robin had become the camp mascot. The counselors had put Sean in charge of caring for it. He'd let me help. It had been kinda neat. But sad, too, when it grew large enough that we had to set it free.

I scrunched up my face. Which he must have liked because his grin got even bigger. How large a smile could he have?

"Okay," I admitted reluctantly. "The bird was cool."

"And how 'bout—"

"Here you go," Ed said, effectively halting our trek down memory lane.

Thank goodness. Being duped into liking a guy who would lie and cheat wasn't exactly my proudest moment.

I stared at the length of rope Ed was dangling in front of us. It was maybe two or two and a half feet long.

"Come on, little lady, take it," he said.

Okay, we *had* turned into a dude ranch while I slept.

"What's it for?" I asked.

"You'll see."

He walked off. I looked at Sean—only because he was the closest person within eye contact.

"Why didn't he give you a rope?" I asked.

Sean shrugged. "Maybe because I'm not a *little lady*."

He did a perfect imitation of Ed, and I couldn't stop myself from smiling.

When Ed had finished passing out the ropes, Edna told us to tie one end around one of partner one's ankles and the other end around one of partner two's ankles. I could see where this was going and it was enough to cause my smile to fade.

She said we were going to do synchronized walking through the woods.

"Sounds like an Olympic event, doesn't it?" Sean asked.

I looked at him, realized I was smiling again, and wiped the smile from my face. I was not going to be charmed by a cheater. "She's got to be kidding."

"Thought we'd already established that she does not kid," Sean said.

And just as he finished speaking, Edna explained that learning to hike through the woods, joined at the ankles, would teach us teamwork.

Sean snatched the rope from my fingers, bent down, and began wrapping and knotting one end around my ankle.

"This is ridiculous," I said. "They're treating us like kids. The whole reason I wanted to be a

CIT was because I'm too old to do this kind of thing."

"It's all part of the team-building mentality," Sean said. "It's like the way you teach a bunch of kids to get along. You give them common goals, something to work on together."

"You say that like you know all about teaching kids."

He peered up at me. He really did have beautiful blue eyes. "I have six younger brothers and sisters."

"You're kidding."

"Unlike Edna, I do believe in joking, but not about that." He began tying the other end of the rope around his ankle. "I've become pretty good at getting them to behave."

"Is that why they chose you to be a CIT?"

"Among other things." He stood up. "I think if we work hard at this we could score a perfect ten."

I thought he was referring to his earlier comment about the synchronized walking Olympic event. I couldn't be sure, though. Something mischievous in his eyes made me wonder if perhaps he was talking about something else. Something more personal.

Like us, maybe, as a couple being a perfect ten. Where did that thought come from?

"Wasn't one of your brothers at camp last year?" I asked.

"Yep. Billy. He's planning to come back this year."

"Brat-Boy," I muttered because he was always getting into mischief. I guess that kind of thing ran in the family.

"Okay, CITs, let's go!" Edna yelled and trudged off in the direction of a worn trail that led into the woods.

"Not fair. She and Ed aren't joined at the ankle," I grumbled.

Sean chuckled.

I started to head for the trail, but my foot got caught. Caught by the rope that Sean had tied to it. I stumbled back, right into his arms.

"So you trust me now to catch you," he said.

"In your dreams."

In *my* dreams. Gosh, he seemed strong. When had that happened? Not that he'd ever held me in his arms before, but, sheesh. I worked my way free of his hold. I noticed we weren't the only ones in an awkward position. The difference was everyone else was laughing, thinking it was funny.

"You need to lighten up," Sean said.

"Are you saying that I'm heavy?" I asked, indignant. I so was not heavy. Maybe I wasn't as thin as Liz — the vegetarian — but I wasn't overweight.

Shaking his head, Sean put his fingers on either side of my mouth and pulled the corners up. "Lighten up. As in your attitude. You are way too serious about this CIT training."

"You know at the end of the week, if we fail—"

"Failure isn't an option." He took a small step and looked back at me. "We just have to work together."

Why was he being so reasonable? And why couldn't I be? Wasn't my ultimate goal not to be sent home by the end of the week? I didn't have to date the guy. I didn't even have to like him.

All I had to do was endure.

I could do that. Easy. No problem.

Actually, once we got into step and adjusted our strides, walking joined at the ankles wasn't too difficult. Of course, I didn't see that it had much potential as an Olympic event.

Sean and I were at the back of the pack. Every now and then, we'd hear a shriek and a grunt as someone stumbled. Embarrassed laughter. Twice I recognized Liz's laughter. I wondered if she was tripping on purpose just to have Terrific Trent help her up.

"So, how 'bout you," Sean suddenly said. "You got any brothers or sisters?"

What was he doing? Picking up a conversation from half an hour ago? I wanted to give him a pointed look or an are-you-a-doofus stare, but I figured any such action on my part would result in my falling into his arms. Literally.

"A brother," I admitted. We were, after all, in the midst of a semi-truce.

"Younger? Older?"

"Younger."

"Name?"

I stopped. He kept going. My leg shot out as he stepped forward.

I teetered. Shrieked.

He spun back. Reached for me.

I dropped to the ground. He fell on top of me. Grunted.

Then he grinned. "We're going to lose some points for this."

"Will you stop with the points already?" I shoved on his shoulders.

He rolled off. I sat up. "Why do you even care what my brother's name is?"

He stood up, careful to keep his foot next to mine to avoid another fall. Then, to my surprise, he reached down and held out his hands.

I thought about being prideful, getting up on my own, but in the end, I put my hands in his and let him pull me to my feet.

Which was a big mistake. Because now we were standing really close. I was wishing he had freckles so I could distract myself with a quick game of connect the freckles. Instead, I had nothing to do except look into his eyes. They were the color of the lake and I felt like I was drowning.

"Four summers," he said quietly. "And I don't know anything about you. Except you paint your toenails a bright red—"

"I don't."

"Gave it up, huh?"

I shook my head. I was so not going to explain myself to him.

"Realized it made you look like a snobby, stuck-up, rich girl—"

I shoved hard on his chest. He yelped, stumbled back—

Which, of course, meant I stumbled on top of him.

A really bad thing. Because I was right on top of him and his arms had wrapped around me, and now we were close enough that he could see the tears in my eyes.

"Oh, great, now you're gonna cry like a baby. Call Edna over and tattle—"

"Jerk!" I hit his shoulder. "I painted my

toenails red that first summer because of my grandmother, okay? She died right before camp started. She always painted her toenails red in summer. The brightest, reddest red she could find. So I did it, too, because I was missing her. So can you shut up already about the toes?"

The shocked look on his face made me think that maybe he was going to shut up for the remainder of the summer. I rolled off him and pushed myself to my feet. Without his help this time, thank you very much.

When he was standing, he said, "Look, Jess, I'm sorry. I didn't know."

Because he'd never asked. I wasn't going to bother to point that out. Besides, it was personal. And four years ago, he'd been nothing except an irritating guy who'd put a snake in my bed.

"Jessica," I said, angling my chin. "Only my friends get to call me Jess."

He grinned. "Trust me. Before summer is over, we're going to be friends."

"No way," I said. I took a giant step forward with my free right foot and tugged on his right foot using my left leg that was roped to him.

"Yes way," he said.

We fell into our synchronized step. Moving quickly to catch up with the others.

Not stumbling once.

It was kinda scary. Like something you would do with a good friend who knew you really well. Knew your steps and your moves.

I had no plans to get serious with Sean. But that didn't mean I was too stubborn to recognize that he was right. That maybe we were not only taking synchronized steps through the woods, but maybe we had just taken a step—a very small step—toward becoming friends.

Chapter Eleven

The next morning, while it was still dark, I got dressed in jeans and a hoodie, grabbed my flashlight, and snuck out of the dormitory. A chill dampness surrounded me as I trudged over the dew-coated ground. I knew I was leaving a vivid trail of footprints that the most inexperienced camper would be able to follow, but I wasn't worried. I wasn't doing anything wrong. I just wanted to check out something.

A heavy stillness hung in the air. One of the things that I really liked about camp was that it was so far away from the city. Well, I'd liked it until I realized that I couldn't get cell phone reception. But even with that drawback, it was still incredibly peaceful out here.

I followed the well-worn path to the lake. When I got to the end of the trail, I turned off my flashlight.

Without the lush canopy of leaves providing a barrier against the first rays of sunlight, I could see clearly. The calm lake. The water lapping at the shore. The wooden dock where I would sometimes come to sit when I needed to be alone. And the old lifeguard platform that was about twenty-five yards from shore. A long, narrow red banner was draped down one side. When the wind blew, the banner waved in the breeze like a flag. This morning no wind stirred.

Lifeguards no longer sat on the platform. Or at least, I'd never seen one sitting there. Campers couldn't go into the water without a head counselor nearby, so we didn't have official lifeguards.

And so the platform was no longer used.

Except as a challenge.

The red banner, a dare.

I'd heard the significance of the red banner the first summer I was here. The first time I'd seen it, it was tied to the porch of the dormitory that I was staying in now.

Until this morning, I'd never actually seen it on the platform. Legend had it that before summer camp officially began, the most courageous counselor would be the first to brave the chilly water of the lake, swim out to the platform, and retrieve the red banner. She would be recognized as the "most outstanding" counselor. The red banner would mark her dormitory. She was given a special cap to distinguish her from everyone else.

From the get-go everyone would know she was special.

I wanted to be seen as special.

I wanted that red banner.

I crouched down at the water's edge and wiggled my fingers in the water.

A shiver went through me. It was cold!

I heard a twig snap and jerked my head around. Sean stood at the edge of the woods, staring at the lake. No, not at the lake. At the platform. At the red banner.

A guy who had wanted to win so badly last year that he'd cheated.

He turned his head slightly, met my gaze. "I'm going after it, Twinkle Toes."

"In what? A canoe?" I called out.

He ambled toward me. "Nah. I'll swim out to get it. That's the rule, isn't it?"

"Since when do you follow rules?"

Ignoring my question, he squatted beside me. "So how cold is it?"

"Pretty cold."

"So why do you want to be the first one to jump in?"

"Why do you?"

"Why not? Someone has to be first."

I stood up. "Well, I've got news for you. It's going to be me, and I'm going to prove it by getting the red banner."

"When?" he asked.

"When you're not looking."

I spun on my heel, started to walk away, then stopped as a horrible thought occurred to me. *Is he going to try to get it now?*

I looked back over my shoulder. He was watching me. "That water is *really* cold right now," I said.

He walked over to me. "I like to win."

"So do I."

"Maybe we should race for it."

I looked at my watch. "We don't have time this morning. They'll be ringing the breakfast bell soon."

"Maybe tomorrow," he said.

Maybe, I thought. But only if he wasn't around.

The tower was huge. Although calling it a tower might give a false impression of what it looked like. It was basically a ladder with a platform on top. And I guess really it only looked huge when you were standing at the top as I was presently doing.

In reality I guess I was about twenty feet off

the ground. I was wearing a harness that was attached to a rope that went over a pulley. I was supposed to jump and trust that the harness, the rope, the pulley, and my partner and the other CITs who were holding the other end of my rope wouldn't let go, would see me safely to the ground.

Liz had leaped off the tower, laughing all the way to the ground. So had Caryn and Torie and Trent and Sean and every other CIT. I'd stayed at the back of the line, hoping rain would come or the sun would fall from the sky. Anything that would stop the other CITs from learning the truth. The truth even my best friend didn't know.

I was a chicken when it came to heights.

Sudden darkness would definitely put an end to Edna's maniacal fun. The woman had this whole trusting-people-to-catch-you issue going on. I figured someone had dropped her as a baby. Why else would she think falling and being caught was the greatest way to establish trust?

I looked at the tops of the trees. Who was I

kidding? I was in the middle of them. I looked at the ground. I envisioned myself as a cartoon character falling. *Splat!*

I trusted that the harness and rope would hold. I trusted that the other CITs had super-human strength and could guide my descent to the ground.

But I didn't trust . . . gravity? What didn't I trust?

This was *Fear Factor* times ten. No, times a hundred.

I couldn't do this.

But I had to do it. I was a CIT. Everyone was waiting.

"It's not jumping," Liz suddenly yelled. "It's flying!"

Did she know about my fears?

"Only chickens don't fly!" Sean suddenly yelled. *"Brawk! Brawk!"*

This jerk was my partner? I'd show him—

And suddenly I wasn't a chicken. I was an eagle! Being lowered to the ground.

My heart was thundering. I could hear it *whoosh, whoosh, whooshing.*

My feet touched the earth. I wanted to do something dramatic like drop to my knees and kiss the dirt. But I was a CIT who'd leaped off a tower. I was cool.

Liz was suddenly hugging me. "See, it wasn't so bad."

No, it wasn't, but I didn't want to do it again. Ever!

That afternoon the rain I'd been praying for while I stood on the tower arrived unexpectedly. Everyone got drenched rushing back to camp.

Edna gave us all an hour to get dried off and over to the activities hut. When I thought of a hut, I thought of something made of straw. This wasn't. It was made of wood, but I guess it seemed adventurous to give different names to the various buildings. It was just another cabin, but it had lots of tables and chairs and artsy stuff, and no one cared if you spilled paint on the floor or tables. Liz and I had done our share of finger painting there, but we figured we wouldn't be doing that today. Finger painting was for campers, not counselors.

Since we were going to be indoors, Liz and I decided to take a little more time to get ready. Liz had smuggled some of her older sister's makeup into her things. The smuggling was a summer camp tradition. Liz's sister owned practically everything Sephora sells, so she never noticed anything was missing. It was the reason we'd been able to have makeover night last year, since neither of our moms would let us wear makeup for real.

And at camp, since we got so hot outdoors, we didn't really want to wear makeup anyway. But the rain changed everything. We put on some mascara and a little blush. Put on the lipstick Liz had confiscated—and took it right off. It was a bright orange that made us both look totally weird.

Since our uniforms were wet, we also had the freedom to wear something that we *wanted* to wear. Because the rain had chilled the air, I put on a long-sleeved fitted hoodie from Abercrombie. It was black with a white flowery-printed design on the front. I put on low-rider jeans. No pierced navel. Mom had let me get my ears pierced when I was ten, but the navel was going to have to wait until I was eighteen. So unfair.

Mom had this thing about me trying to grow up too fast. If she had her way I'd be a kid forever.

Slipping on my flip-flops, I looked down at my bare toenails and thought of my grandma. But I didn't have time to do the nails justice. Besides, I'd be splashing through water on the way to the activities hut anyway. I slipped on the bright yellow rain poncho that we were required to bring to camp.

Liz, Caryn, and Torie were all wearing theirs as well.

"I hate these things," Torie said, tugging on her poncho. "You know what I'm saying?"

"Better than an umbrella," Caryn said.

We pranced our way over to the activities hut, trying to avoid the puddles that were growing bigger and bigger as the rain continued to fall. Of course the guys were standing on the porch beneath the overhang, laughing like they'd never seen anyone running through the rain.

Weren't only mature guys supposed to be selected as CITs?

Inside the building was nice, warm, and best of all, dry. We hung our ponchos on the pegs beside the door.

"You think we'll do face painting?" Liz asked.

"We're not campers," I said. "We're CITs."

"True. So what do you think we'll do?"

"Climb on a table and fall off?" I asked.

"Can you do a table, or will you freeze up again?"

"I was kidding," I said.

"So what was happening with you earlier?" Liz asked. "You looked terrified."

Great. So much for thinking I was masking my true feelings.

"I'm just not into jumping off high things."

"I didn't know that," she said.

"It's not something I really like to talk about."

"But I'm your best friend. Didn't you trust me?"

"It wasn't a matter of trust, it was just . . . embarrassing. Don't you have any secret fears?" I asked.

"Yeah. That Trent won't like me as much as I like him. I'm really starting to crush on him, Jess. It's kinda scary."

Neither of us had ever had a boyfriend before, so all the feelings that come from liking someone and him actually liking you back were kind of strange. Or at least I figured they would be. I didn't like anyone at the moment and certainly didn't have anyone liking me.

"How can he not like you enough? You're awesome."

"You only think that because you're my best friend."

"I think it because it's true. Besides, remember when we took that quiz in *Teen People* a few months back? According to that, we're both ready for a serious boyfriend."

"Yeah, but you and I always do well on quizzes. You know, I really do wish we'd do face painting. I wouldn't mind painting a heart on Trent's cheek."

"I'm sure Terrific Trent would love that."

"Hey, I might even be willing to paint Sean's cheek."

"You're kidding me."

"No, I'd put a 'stay away from my best friend' sign."

I rolled my eyes. "He can't, though. We're partners."

"And getting to be cozy partners at that. He knew how to get you to jump off that tower. He knew you a lot better than I did. Be careful, Jess. He's going to make you like him and then he'll betray you. You can't trust him."

"I *don't* trust him."

"Hey, partner," Sean said.

I wondered how much of the conversation he'd heard. But it didn't really matter because I'd only spoken the truth, and he knew exactly how I felt anyway.

"I think we're going to get the afternoon away from each other," I said.

"No such luck," Sean said. "At least a hundred different team-building activities can be done indoors."

"Why do you know so much about team building?"

"Because I researched the activities. They're great for keeping the brats at home under control when I have to babysit."

"The brats? That's a nice way to refer to your family."

"Hey, you try taking care of six—"

"We'll be taking care of a lot more than that in another week."

"But we won't be related to them."

"And that makes a difference?"

"You bet. They can't start screaming, 'I'm gonna tell Mom.'"

I laughed. Sean grinned. "I finally said something you like."

I shook my head. "It's just that every conversation with Alex starts that way."

"Alex is your brother?"

"Yeah."

"I bet he's a total pain."

For the first time in my life I felt a need to defend my brother. He was, in fact, a pain, but it seemed a betrayal to admit it to Sean. "He's okay."

"So you have a younger brother named Alex. See, it only took me two days to find that out. By the end of summer, I'll know all your secrets."

"Why do you even care?" I asked.

He seemed surprised by the question. "Because you're my partner."

"Only for the week, Sean. Then we'll never have to hang out again. I don't hang with cheaters."

"What if I had a good reason for what I did?"

I stared at him. "You did have a reason, but it wasn't a good one. You wanted to win."

"Another reason."

"Like you wanted me to lose?"

"Forget it."

Edna blew her whistle. And following her instructions, our little circle of two—Sean and me—grew to include Liz and Trent. Each group had to stand in front of an easel. It had a huge pad of paper on it because it was used for all kinds of artwork and projects.

"This exercise is called 'Marooned,'" Edna said. "You're going to be stranded on a desert island. I want your team to list five items the team would have with it if you thought you might be marooned. You've got five minutes. Go!"

She clicked her stopwatch. Geez, just like my hand curled in permanent cell-phone-holding position, her stopwatch seemed to be her handheld device of choice.

"Okay, water," Trent said and wrote it on our tablet of paper.

"No, way," Liz said. "We're on an island. There's plenty of water."

"Could be salt water," Trent said.

"But fresh water is bound to be somewhere

on the island," Sean said. "Or we could harvest rain."

"How would we harvest rain?" I asked.

"We'll have to figure that out later," Liz said. "We only have five minutes." She crossed out water.

It was a little strange to see Liz taking charge. I didn't know if she was doing it to impress Trent or if she was really getting into the whole leadership thing. Maybe it was a little of both.

"A gun," Trent said.

"We can build traps with whatever the landscape has to offer," Sean said.

I looked at him. "You're really into nature."

He grinned. "I'm into survival."

"The John Locke of CLS," Trent said, referring to a character on *Lost*.

"That works for me," Sean said.

"So what do we need?" I asked, practically hearing the seconds ticking away on Edna's stopwatch. "Cell phone is useless. We can't even get a signal here."

"A hunting knife," Sean said.

Sounded reasonable. I wrote it on the paper.

"Matches," Trent said.

Sean nodded. "So we could have signal fires."

"You're assuming we want to be found," Liz said. "Maybe being marooned is the best thing to happen to us. No school, no parents. Totally on our own."

"We could use a fire for other things," I said. "Like cooking the food we catch in traps and keeping warm."

"Chocolate," Liz said suddenly, totally taking our list to a new level. "We gotta have chocolate."

Feeling like being silly, I wrote it down. I no longer cared what Edna thought. This exercise was pointless. We were never going to be marooned.

"You're not taking our list seriously," Trent said.

"Not really, no," Liz said.

"Okay. Then I want my iPod Shuffle."

"Done," I said. *This is actually getting to be fun*, I thought.

"Red nail polish," Sean said.

I jerked my head around and stared at him.

"Why would you take *that*?" Trent asked as though Sean had suggested we take dog poop.

Sean smiled. "So Twinkle Toes here will be happy."

Whenever he'd called me Twinkle Toes before, it had made me angry. But it didn't this time. I didn't know why. Maybe because he hadn't said it like it was a put-down.

"Time!" Edna called.

We all looked at each other, then at our list. I was sorta wishing Liz hadn't crossed out gun. As far as working as a team, we were pretty pitiful. We were going to be stranded on a deserted island eating chocolate, painting our toenails, listening to music by a fire while Sean cut things up. *Great. Just great.*

Edna made the rounds, reading aloud everyone's survival list. It was interesting. It seems that surviving wasn't the point. Agreeing on our list was.

So maybe I was going to make it as a counselor after all.

Question thirteen: *"Do you know how to compromise?"*

Check!

XOXOX   Chapter Twelve

B y Thursday all the leadership training and learning to work together seemed to be getting us somewhere. I just wasn't sure where. Since the "Marooned" exercise, our two-person teams had morphed into permanent four-person teams. Liz, Trent, Sean, and me. We were even eating our meals together. Although Sean being there might have been by default.

I mean, I didn't actually invite Sean to join us, but Trent was hanging really closely to Liz, and she was all about being with him. I couldn't believe how well they got along. Talk about partnering up.

Liz and I had spent the spring researching games for our campers to play and craft projects to keep them entertained on rainy days. I wanted to be the best counselor ever.

I'd thought my partner in all this would be Liz. Not Sean.

And I hated to admit that he was a little interesting. And sometimes funny.

"You know, we made a big mistake with our 'Marooned' list," Sean said now, as we were sitting at the breakfast table.

"Yeah?" Trent said, around a mouthful of bacon.

The food was buffet style, all you could eat. For the CITs anyway. For now. Once camp got underway, it would all be limited to one helping. Otherwise they'd run out of food quickly because guy campers could eat a lot!

Sean punched his fork into his pancake and lifted it. "We should have added CLS's pancakes to our list of things we'd want with us on a deserted island. These things are rubbery enough we could probably use them to build a raft."

"They are pretty bad," Trent said. "But they're better than my mom's. She can't cook at all."

"My mom was a really good cook," Sean said.

"Was?" I asked.

He looked over at me like he'd said something he wished he hadn't. "She died a few years back."

"I'm sorry."

"My dad remarried last year. Kate. She has three kids. We're a regular *Yours, Mine, and Ours* family."

"That movie was so bad," Liz said, like his reference to a movie was the most important thing he'd said.

"That must have been hard," I said.

"Watching that movie was one of the hardest things I've ever done," Liz said. "Honestly,

I almost had to get up and leave. Remember how we—"

"Liz," I said, cutting her off, wondering when in the last few days she'd lost the ability to read my mind. It was like Trent had messed up our being in sync. "I wasn't talking about the movie."

"Oh, sorry."

"No big deal," Sean said. "I adjusted. Being able to come to camp every summer really helped. Both after I lost my mom and when I got a new mom."

I wondered if his new family had messed him up. If he'd felt a need to cheat because he'd felt a need to win.

"Billy . . ." I said slowly, trying to remember. "I don't remember him coming before last summer."

"Last summer was his first time. Dad thought it would help us bond. I had two younger sisters, Billy had two baby sisters. Neither of us was used to having a brother around."

"Did it help?" I asked, wondering why I

suddenly cared. Was I just feeling sorry for him?

"Not really. But like I said, no big deal."

Only I was starting to wonder if it had been a big deal.

After breakfast, we had a session on first aid. How to stanch the flow of blood. How to stabilize a broken arm. We were all given small first aid kits that we were supposed to start carrying in our backpack at all times.

Then we broke for lunch, with instructions to ready ourselves for an intense hike in the woods, a lesson on survival.

Knowing Edna, it would include a lesson on trust as well. I wondered what she was going to have us fall off of now.

"So what do you think is up with the survival hike?" Liz asked.

"It must be dangerous," Torie said. "Why else give us the first aid training first? You know what I'm saying?"

I did know what she was saying, but I figured

she was overreacting. "They're not going to put us in a truly dangerous situation," I said. "But we need to know what to do in case we take the younger campers hiking. So they'll teach us how to avoid poison ivy and snakes. It's no big deal."

"Actually," Jon said, "last year one of the counselors told me that training got kinda hairy at the end. That their trainers took them out into the woods and left them."

"Like what? Hansel and Gretel?" Caryn asked.

He shrugged. "I guess."

"Why would they do that?" I asked.

"Why do they do any of this stuff?" Trent asked.

"So we learn to rely on each other, trust each other," Sean said.

"I don't think leaving us out in the woods would accomplish that," I said.

"They mentioned survival," Liz reminded me.

"So I'll pack water, my flashlight, and my cell phone," I said.

"Like our cell phones will do us any good," Liz said.

Before we headed out, Edna and Ed had made our two-person CIT teams count off. Sean and I were Team Eight. I wasn't certain how we always ended up being last, but for some reason we did.

And that was kinda cool because being in the back put us far away from Edna and Ed who were leading the group. It meant we were less likely to get into trouble.

I took my cell phone out of my pocket and turned it on. "No signal," I muttered.

"Could be the trees," Sean said.

"That's what Liz thought," I said. "I think it has to do with how far away we are from anything remotely civilized."

"Why would you want to call and talk with anyone when you have me to talk to?" Sean asked.

I pointed the camera at him and clicked a picture. Now why did I do that? Now I not only had Sean walking beside me but proof of his existence in my camera. It was easy enough to delete the picture . . . only I didn't.

I told myself that as much as I disliked him, he was a camp memory. *Right, Jess.* The truth was, over the past few days he'd grown on me. Not enough that I trusted him completely. Not enough that I was entirely comfortable with liking him. But enough that I thought if the past four summers had never happened, if I'd met him for the first time this summer, that I might be crushing on him like Liz was crushing on Trent.

That was a scary thought.

"Did you just take a picture of me?" he asked.

"No, the fauna behind you," I lied. Now who was a liar? I took a picture of Liz and Trent trudging in front of us. They were walking so closely together I was surprised they didn't bump into each other.

I took a picture of one of the trees.

"That's a cool phone," Sean said. "Can I see it?"

"Sure." I handed it to him.

He snapped a picture of me. "E-mail it to me when you get home," he said, grinning.

I took my camera back. "I'll have better things to do," I said. Although I wasn't sure what they would be. I glanced over at him. "I'll see."

Ed and Edna called for a stop.

"Team One!" Edna called out, which seemed silly to me since Team One was standing right in front of her. But I figured she had a point to make.

She removed a handful of bandannas from her backpack.

"All week we've been preparing you for this moment," she said. "The moment of absolute trust. We're going to take each team to a different drop-off point. One team member will be blindfolded and led back to camp by the other team member."

I stared at the bandanna she'd handed me. Was this a hint that I was supposed to be the blindfolded team member? That I was supposed to trust Sean to lead me back to camp?

"Team One, you'll head back from here,"

she said. "Teams Three, Five, and Seven, follow me. The rest of you follow Ed."

Liz spun around and looked at me, looked at Sean. She gave me a weak smile. "See you back at camp."

"Right," I said. "Good luck."

She and Trent hurried to catch up with Edna.

"This way," Ed said, indicating a path that went in the opposite direction from the one Edna had taken.

"Aren't you worried that we'll all get lost?" I asked as I fell into step behind him and the others.

"Nah, little lady. I'm not going to take you that far off the beaten path. All you'll have to do is yell really loudly and I'll find you."

I was actually quite proud of myself. Not once during the entire trek, as Ed released one group after another to find their way back, did I make a sarcastic comment about trust. Mainly because I was spending a great deal of time thinking that if I was blindfolded, Sean would be leading me. Holding my arm. Walking really, really close to me.

And if I was leading him . . .

To keep myself distracted from those thoughts, I kept taking pictures of all the interesting things we passed. A rabbit hiding in the brush. A web with a humongous spider on it. An occasional brightly colored flower.

Finally, it was just Sean and me.

"Figure out who is going to lead who," Ed said. He patted my shoulder. "Good luck getting back."

He walked off.

"That had an ominous ring to it," Sean said.

"I can't believe they're just leaving us out here."

"Honestly? I don't think we're that far from camp. He was circling around, trying to make us think we'd walked a long way." He shrugged, pointed. "But it's just over there. Go ahead and cover your eyes with the bandanna."

I stared at him. "And why do I get to be blindfolded?"

144

"Because I was paying attention to where we were going, while you were distracted taking pictures."

"Sean—"

"I know. You don't trust me. The thing is, Jessica, I don't trust you, either. Not when it comes to following a trail that you weren't paying any attention to."

That hurt. I couldn't believe how much it hurt. To not be trusted. I didn't deserve that. I hadn't done anything to earn his not trusting me.

I turned around, looked at the area where Ed had disappeared. No toilet paper to mark the path.

Sighing, I pulled the bandanna through my fingers.

"Come on, Jessica," Sean said. "It'll be getting dark soon."

I looked over at him. "You know the way back?"

He nodded.

What did I have to lose? And who knew?

Maybe I'd gain something. I tied the bandanna around my head so my eyes were covered.

"All right, Sean," I said. "Prove to me that I can trust you."

Chapter Thirteen

"We're lost! I don't freaking believe this!" I turned around slowly. Nothing looked familiar. But then I wasn't on a first-name basis with trees. And that's all that surrounded me. Big, towering trees.

I saw no trail, no lake, no cabins.

No sunlight. Only the dim glow of Sean's flashlight. It was night!

"I'm not believing this," I repeated. I glared at Sean. "Why didn't you say something sooner?"

"Because I thought I'd find the way," he said, seriously irritated.

I couldn't figure out why he was irritated. I was the one who had trusted him. . . . Whoa! No, I hadn't completely trusted him. And my lack of trust was apparently well deserved.

"What now, Daniel Boone?" I asked. I plopped down on a hollow log. "Weren't we supposed to be back before dark?"

"Yeah."

"So you think they're looking for us?"

"I don't know."

I looked at him suspiciously. "This isn't one of your tricks, is it? You know, like the snake in my bed?"

"I wish."

He sounded seriously bummed out.

I worked my backpack off my shoulders and removed the water bottle from the side pocket. I drank some water and then held the bottle out to Sean.

He shook his head.

"Look, you don't want to get dehydrated," I said.

"I'll take some when I'm really thirsty."

"Fine." I put the bottle back. Then I flicked

my wrist to turn on the indigo light on my dad's watch and looked at the compass. "Do you even know if we need to go north or south?"

"Not really."

I glared at him. "My mom always gives my dad a hard time, saying that men have this gene that prevents them from asking for directions." I shook my head. "You should have told me we were lost. I could have taken the blindfold off earlier and helped you figure out where we were."

"That would have been cheating," he said absently, looking around the small clearing.

I stared at him, knocked the side of my head a couple of times, pretending to clear water out of my ears. "Excuse me? Cheating Sean was worried about cheating?"

"Can you get over that already? I told you I've changed."

"You also said you had a good reason for doing what you did. Well, I can't think of a better reason than survival. But this afternoon, you wouldn't cheat? Explain that one, Einstein."

He said nothing. But it made no sense. He

would cheat to win a game, but not to survive?

He started gathering up limbs and sticks. Then he put them in the middle of the clearing.

"Are you going to build a fire?" I asked.

"Just a little one. Maybe someone will see it. If nothing else, it'll keep us warm."

Not that it was really cold or anything, but it was a bit cooler than it had been earlier in the day. And having a fire would allow us to turn off our flashlights and save our battery power. Who knew what the night would bring or when we might get rescued or find our way back to camp?

I shoved myself to my feet and began to help him. We worked in silence for a long time, until we had a pile of dried branches, leaves, and twigs in place, surrounded by a tight ring of rocks so the fire wouldn't spread. Sean crouched down and began rubbing two twigs together.

I'd always heard about people starting fires by rubbing two sticks together, but watching Sean, I realized it was a lot of work, and sparks didn't instantly appear.

"Do you know what you're doing?" I asked.

"Sorta. Friction is supposed to create heat that will start a fire."

I reached into my backpack and took out a small box of matches. I struck a match and lit the leaves we'd placed beneath some twigs. They caught fire immediately. By the time they'd burned, the smaller twigs were flaming.

I figured that, before long, we'd have a full-fledged campfire.

Sean dropped back. He didn't look too happy. "You could have told me you had matches."

"You could have told me we were lost."

He withdrew a stick from the pile before it caught fire and began to make X's on the ground. "I was embarrassed, okay? I knew you didn't trust me to get you back to camp. I wanted to prove . . ." His voice trailed off. He sighed.

What did he want to prove? That he could be trusted? Had he really changed that much? I hated to admit that, if not for last summer, I might have developed a serious crush on this guy. He was cute, seemed nice, dependable, made me smile, and sometimes made me laugh. But I'd fallen for that routine before.

Still, I felt really bad that, for whatever reason, he'd tried to go it alone. "I've got a great sense of direction," I said lamely.

"I know. That's the reason your team always wins Capture the Flag."

"Is that why you cheated?" I asked.

He didn't say anything, but that wasn't a good reason: jealousy. But weren't cheaters and liars the same? Could you have one without the other?

"Maybe if I climb a tree I'll be able to see the lights of our dormitory," I suggested.

Sean stood up. "That's a good idea, but I thought you were afraid of heights."

"I'm not too crazy about jumping from heights. But I can climb a tree. No sweat."

Only none of the branches were low enough for me to reach. It was my being vertically challenged interfering again. I knew without even pondering it that Sean was going to climb a tree. Just hop up and go.

And that irritated me.

He reached for a branch.

"It was my idea," I said.

Sean stared at me over his shoulder. "So? You can't reach a branch and I can."

"Boost me up."

"You're going to trust me to boost you up?"

Did I trust him? It was strange. I didn't trust *him*, but I did trust that at this point he'd do whatever he needed to in order to get us out of this. At least now that survival was a real issue, and he'd realized the error of his ways. But even *I* separated trust of the person from trust of his actions. Trust of the person went so much deeper. And I wasn't ready to trust Sean that much.

"You want to survive as much as I do," I said.

"We're not in a life-threatening situation," he said.

"Still, like I said, it was my idea. So help me up."

"You like to be in charge, don't you? Why is

being the one to win so important to you?" he asked.

Ignoring his question, I slapped my hand on the tree. "Help me up."

He linked his hands together and bent slightly. I put my foot on his palms, my hands on the tree to steady myself. He hoisted me up. I grabbed a branch, pulled myself up.

Why was winning important to me?

Because I'd wanted to play on the basketball team in middle school, but I was told that I couldn't because I wasn't tall enough. I wanted to run track, but the coach said my legs weren't long enough and I couldn't run fast enough. But here at camp, I could slip through the woods quietly. I could capture a flag.

Unless someone cheated.

I worked my way up the tree, ignoring the pain as the bark scraped my shins and knees. Yes, I wanted to win. I wanted to prove I was the best. But was I so set on winning that I made everyone else feel bad about losing?

Why hadn't Sean told me we were lost sooner?

I stopped climbing as the truth hit me.

Because he hadn't trusted *me*. He hadn't trusted me not to make him feel bad, not to make fun of him. He hadn't trusted me to be his true partner.

We're a great team, I thought sarcastically.

I'd been so caught up in not trusting him that I hadn't realized that maybe he couldn't trust me, either.

"See anything?" he asked.

A lot more than I wanted to see, but what I was looking at was inside rather than outside.

I started climbing down the tree. When I hit the ground, I said, "Nothing."

"Nothing at all?"

"Nope."

"We can't be that far from camp."

"Apparently, we are."

"Great," he said. "That's just great. I really screwed up. I'm sorry, Jessica."

"Jess," I said. "Only my mom calls me Jessica."

"I thought only your friends called you Jess."

Ignoring his statement, I sat on the ground and pulled my backpack into my lap. "I've got a granola bar. Want half?"

"Sure. I'm starving."

I smiled.

"What?" he asked.

"I'm thinking about that 'Marooned' list we had to make." I opened the granola bar, broke it in half, and generously gave him the larger half. So technically it wasn't cut in half.

"Yeah, I could use a knife right about now," he muttered.

I chuckled. "What would you do with it? Skin a bear?"

He shrugged. "Whittle."

"You know how to whittle?"

"Yeah, my granddad taught me. I whittle whenever I miss him. It's kinda like painting your toenails, I guess."

Gosh, it was scary to think we might be

more alike than I realized.

"I was thinking about the chocolate," I said, as I bit off a bit of granola bar.

He laughed. "You want chocolate right now?"

"Yeah."

"Chicks. You don't take survival seriously."

"Hey, I climbed the tree."

He grinned. "Yeah, you did."

"We just have to survive the night," I said, speaking more bravely than I felt. "We'll find our way back to camp tomorrow."

"At least there are no bears," he said.

I drew my legs up to my chest and wrapped my arms around my shins, careful to avoid the scrapes. They didn't look too bad in the firelight.

"So why do you want to be a counselor?" he asked.

"Because I like to be the boss. How about you? Taking care of a bunch of kids at camp can't be that much different than taking care of your brothers and sisters."

He shrugged. "It's different watching out

for them at camp. I'm not doing it alone."

I drew my brows together. "I know Billy was here. Were your sisters here, too?"

"Nah, just Billy."

"I remember him."

"In your nightmares?"

I grinned. "He wasn't that bad. Is he going to be here this summer?"

"Yeah, first session."

"Bonding again?"

"I don't think so. They won't put relatives in the same group."

The truth dawned, and I unwound my arms. "You want to be a counselor because you don't want to bond with him."

"It's not that I don't *want* to bond with him. I just . . ." He sighed. "I just think it would be easier on him if he didn't feel like I was watching him all the time."

"I can dig that."

"You know, who wants big brother watching?"

"Right." I scrounged through my backpack,

came up with a melted mint. I wondered how old it was. I dropped it back inside. "Don't you have any food?" I asked.

"Nope."

I leaned back against a tree. "It's going to be a long night. Maybe we should at least try to find the camp."

"If I couldn't find it in the light, I don't see how we'll find it in the dark," he said.

He had a point.

"Have you heard that Ed and Edna are twins?" I asked.

"Yeah, but you already told us that Ed says they're not."

"Exactly, so then what are they? Do you think maybe Ed's her son?"

Sean laughed. "I don't think that's it. They look about the same age."

"Do you think they could be married?"

"That would explain the matching rings on their left hand."

Matching rings? How had I missed that?

I was disappointed that we'd figured it out

so quickly. I was looking for something that would challenge me through the night, keep me awake and alert. Something to keep my mind off the fact that we were lost.

Normally I loved the woods, but it was kinda creepy being in the woods at night with only Sean. Not that Sean was creepy, but the woods were so quiet, except for an occasional owl hooting. Once I heard a rush of wings and then a squeal. I didn't want to contemplate what might be going on there. I was all for survival of the fittest, but I had a weak spot for small creatures. Came from being a small creature myself.

"Should we take shifts keeping watch?" I asked.

"You're going to trust me to watch over you?"

"Never mind. Bad idea. But if you want to sleep . . ."

"I don't."

I thought about saying that I might trust him a little —

"Do you want to know what time it is in Japan?" I asked to keep myself from confessing something I might regret.

"Nah, that's okay. Cool watch, though."

"Thanks. It's my dad's."

We both sat there for a while, not saying anything. The night got really quiet, except for the bugs chirping.

"Jess?" he said after a while. "I don't blame you for not trusting me . . . what with the snake and all, but that first summer . . . I was just trying to get your attention."

I jerked my head around and stared at him. "What?"

"I thought you were cute. I wanted you to notice me."

"With a snake?"

He grinned, shrugged. "I was ten. Romance wasn't exactly in my vocabulary."

I picked up a stick, started scratching at the dirt. "I thought you were cute back then."

"Really?"

"Yeah."

"Would flowers have worked better than a snake?"

I laughed, actually laughed. "Most definitely.

Chocolate even better."

He chuckled, then got really quiet. "We'll be at the same high school next year."

"If we survive tonight."

"Yeah," he said solemnly. "If we survive tonight."

Chapter Fourteen

XOXOX

I didn't remember falling asleep. One minute I was staring into the fire, and then . . .

I wasn't.

I jerked awake, disoriented and aching, as though I'd spent the night sleeping on the ground.

Oh, wait. I *had* spent the night sleeping on the ground. Yawning, I struggled to sit up. The fire was gone, but we weren't in darkness, because dawn was arriving.

I looked over and Sean was asleep, too.

Some guard he turned out to be.

I couldn't believe that he'd told me that he'd liked me that first summer. Or that he'd thought he could get my attention with a snake!

How lame was that?

Guys. Honestly. They were cute. And they were fun. And I wanted a boyfriend more than anything . . . but sometimes guys did the goofiest things for the silliest reasons.

Like switching out a map just so his team could win.

I remembered how the lead counselor, Hank, had made everyone gather in front of the main lodge. He'd held up the fake map and wanted to know who was responsible for it.

We'd all known it was someone on the other team, and so we'd all waited. I remembered that I'd started being interested in Sean again. We'd set the bird free two days before and had kinda bonded over that.

I'd looked through the crowd trying to find Sean . . . he was talking to Billy. Billy, who was his new brother. And Sean had looked mad.

Then he'd stepped forward and announced, "I did it."

Sean, who had nursed a baby bird back to health. Who had taken such good care of it. Sean, who I had seen more than once giving attention to Billy, talking to him, trying to be his friend as well as his new big brother.

Sean, who wanted to be a counselor so he wouldn't be in charge of his brother this year.

Sean's eyes suddenly opened. He grinned. "Hey, Twinkle Toes."

"You're a liar," I said quietly. "Not a cheater."

His brow furrowed as he sat up. "What?"

"Let's play a game of Truth or Dare," I said.

He yawned. "No way. It's daylight. We need to try to find our way back to the dormitory."

"Tell the truth or take a dare," I said.

He shook his head. "Not playing."

"Come on, Sean. One question each."

"I'll take a dare every time, Jess."

"Because you're afraid I'll learn the truth

about the map. You know I'll ask about the map."

"I don't know, and I don't care." He stood up.

I scrambled to my feet. "You didn't swap out the maps. Your brother did. And you lied to protect him. I remember you were talking to him—"

"Let it go, Jess."

"I'm right," I stated emphatically.

"What does it matter?"

"Why would you let me think you were a cheater?"

"Because that's what big brothers do."

"No, it's not."

"I'm supposed to look out for him."

And I realized that, before Sean's dad remarried, Sean had never been a big brother to a little brother. To sisters, yes, but not to a brother. He'd been trying to protect Billy.

"Will you at least confirm that I'm right? I won't tell anyone. I just . . . I just always liked you, Sean. Even when you put a snake in my bed.

"And then you confessed to cheating, and it

wasn't so much that my team lost . . . it was that I'd started to really like a guy who could do something like that. So not only didn't I think I could trust you, but how could I trust my own judgment?"

He dropped his head back, stared at the sky that was beginning to lighten. "You have to promise not to tell."

"I promise."

"He did some other things last summer. They said if he got into trouble one more time, they'd send him home. He was just a kid, acting out, angry because suddenly he had a dad and an older brother, and he wasn't the oldest anymore, wasn't the one in charge." He shrugged. "At least that's what the family counselor said."

"So you took the blame so they wouldn't send him home?"

"Yeah. And so they'd let him come back this summer. Summer camp is the absolute best. And Billy has changed a lot. Like I said, family counselor. He had some anger issues. But he's basically a good kid."

And Sean Reed?

My instincts had been right. I shouldn't have stopped trusting them.

I dangled the blindfold that I'd been wearing the day before. "Maybe you should wear this today."

"Maybe we should work together."

"Don't you trust me?" I asked.

"Jess, seriously. We are way lost." He looked around. His brow furrowed. "Does any of this look familiar to you?"

I glanced around. "A little maybe."

"I think we're back where Ed dropped us off."

"I'm not sure that information helps us much."

He spun around. "You still have the pictures on your phone that you took yesterday?"

"Why wouldn't I have them?"

"You can delete them, right?"

"I can, but I didn't."

"Great. Show me the last one you took."

I pulled out my phone, brought up the picture. Sean looked at it over my shoulder, standing really close to me. That little electric charge went through my body again.

"There's Ed," he said slowly. "Why would you take a picture of Ed?"

"I was crushing on him."

He looked horrified. "Seriously?"

"No! But he's part of the camp experience. I like to document my experiences."

"Right." He looked back at the picture. "The tree he was standing in front of is . . . right there."

He pointed across the clearing. Then he spun me around, grinning broadly. "All we have to do is look at your pictures backward and find the same landmarks."

I narrowed my eyes. "Is that cheating?"

"It's genius, Jess. You're a genius. You discovered a way to mark a trail that's better than bread crumbs."

"I don't know if I'd go that far," I said. "But it doesn't really matter. Let's go."

We walked until we found the next spot I'd taken a picture of.

"I don't understand how we got so lost yesterday," I said. "You should have had the sun to keep you oriented. It's not like you're in the jungles of a rain forest or anything."

"I wasn't in any hurry to get back to camp," he said.

"I don't understand. Once we got back to camp, we'd have the rest of the afternoon to goof off."

I saw his jaw tighten. "And you would have goofed off with Liz."

"Yeah, so?"

"You're really thick, Jess."

Like an ancient tree.

"You *wanted* to spend the time with *me*?"

He stopped walking. "Is that so hard to believe?"

I stepped back and leaned against a tree. "So were you working up the courage to tell me you weren't a cheat?"

He leaned back against another tree. "I was

never going to tell you that."

"Because you didn't trust me to keep the secret?"

"Because *you* don't trust me. You would have just thought I was lying, trying to score points."

I nodded, looked down at my hiking boots, my scraped shins. Scary how alike we were. "Can we agree to be totally honest with each other from now on?"

"Not totally," he said. "I've got secrets."

"Like what?" I asked.

"If I told you, it wouldn't be a secret."

"You're crushing on Edna, aren't you?" I asked as I pushed myself away from the tree.

"I'm crushing on someone," he admitted.

My heart skipped a beat, maybe two, while I watched him shove himself away from the tree. "Let's see the next picture," he said.

I brought the next picture up on the screen, and we started comparing the surrounding area.

"I think this bush is that bush," Sean said,

pointing west, according to my compass.

"Yeah, you're right."

It was kinda strange to work with Sean instead of against him. To cooperate.

It was strange but also nice.

He did have a killer smile. The most beautiful blue eyes.

And if I was honest with myself—which I usually was—I admired what he'd done for his brother. I wasn't convinced it had been the best thing for Billy, but who was I to judge? Alex had been my brother since the day he was born. I didn't know what it felt like to suddenly find yourself with three extra sibs.

To try to be an older brother to a younger brother.

"Hey, this is really starting to look familiar," Sean said. He took a deep breath. "I think I smell bacon."

"Here, take my camera," I said.

"I don't think we're going to need it anymore," he said. "I'm pretty sure the main camp is . . . Hey, what are you doing?"

I was wrapping the bandanna around my head. "You're supposed to lead me back to camp."

I felt his hand circle my wrist. He pulled the bandanna away from my eyes.

"I'm not going to take credit for something I didn't do," he said. "We did this as a team."

I smiled at him. I'd really been hoping he'd say that, but I'd been willing to give him the credit if he wanted it. Although what I was starting to feel for him would have come to a grinding halt. Instead I felt it expanding. Scary.

Before I could say anything, I heard a scream and then—

"You're back!"

I spun around. Liz ran to me, nearly knocked me over, and hugged me tightly.

"I was so worried!" She leaned back, looked me in the eye. "Are you okay? I wanted to form a search party, but Edna said you were all right—"

"How did Edna know we were okay?" Sean asked.

"I don't know. She said Ed was with you."

"Ed?" Sean and I asked at the same time.

"He wasn't with us," I said.

Then I heard whistling. I looked up the path along which Sean and I had trekked.

And there was Ed, ambling toward us.

"Learned to work together, I see," Ed said as he walked by.

"Did you know where we were?" Sean asked.

Ed stopped walking. "Yep. Kept an eye on you all night."

"Why didn't you say something?" I asked, seriously ticked. "Help us get back here?"

"You were supposed to get yourselves back here." He winked at us. "And you did."

He walked on to the dining hall.

I looked at Sean. "I guess we were never in serious trouble."

"You sound disappointed," he said.

"I thought we'd survived, that we'd done it on our own."

"We did do it on our own."

But that wasn't exactly right. I looked at him and smiled. "Come to think of it, I guess we did it together."

Chapter Fifteen

Sean and I weren't hailed as heroes or anything. As a matter of fact, most of the CITs razzed us because we hadn't made it back to camp the evening before. That we'd gotten lost.

Sean liked to say that we were just delayed.

And I thought maybe that was the truth. He'd taken us on a detour, so we'd have a little more time together, so maybe I would come to know him a little better.

The fact that Ed had been acting as our

guardian—unbeknownst to us—really didn't change anything.

Sean and I had finally bonded.

"I can't believe you and Sean didn't kill each other," Liz said while I was eating breakfast. She'd eaten earlier but had decided to join me in the dining hall to hear the details of my night alone with Sean.

Apparently, Trent, Jon, and Jet wanted Sean's version of events because they'd ushered him off to another table for some guy talk.

"Do you like him now?" Liz asked.

I bit off a bit of bacon, chewed slowly, and thought about how I should answer that question. "I no longer don't like him."

She furrowed her brow. "So you're saying you like him."

I nodded. It was easier than admitting the truth with words.

"So what happened?" she asked quietly, leaning closer to me. "Did he kiss you?"

"No, we just talked."

"About what?"

"Different things. Nothing important."

"But now you like him?"

I glanced over at the table where Sean was sitting. I had a feeling I wasn't going to be experiencing any more practical jokes. He looked over at me, winked, and smiled.

"Yeah," I said to Liz, taking a deep breath so I could say the words. "Yeah, I like him."

The next morning, I woke up early, just as the sun was coming up, got dressed, and walked down to the lake. It was our last day of training. Tomorrow the first group of campers would arrive.

The red banner was still hanging limply from the lifeguard platform. No one had tried to get it. At least not that I'd heard of.

I walked out to the edge of the dock. I sat with my legs crossed beneath me. Stared at the banner. Wondered if only the top of the water was cold, if it would feel warm after I'd been in it for a while. If I could reach the platform before I froze to death.

"Painting your toenails?" a voice asked.

I looked over my shoulder. Sean was walking toward the dock. Swaggering, really. Like he thought he was some tough guy. His shirt was unbuttoned, and it looked like he was wearing swim trunks.

Which was fine. Beneath my hoodie and shorts, I was wearing a bathing suit.

"No," I said as he crouched down beside me. "Not painting my toenails."

He looked toward the lifeguard platform, the red banner. "You gonna go for it?"

"I don't know. I'm thinking about it."

"That morning when I saw you out here, you said you thought I'd cheat to get the banner. How was I going to cheat?"

I was a little embarrassed now to realize how much I'd mistrusted him. "I thought you'd row out in a canoe, get the banner, then stand under a warm shower until you got wet." I shrugged. "Tell people you'd jumped into the lake."

"Man, you really do have some trust issues where I'm concerned."

I bit my lip. "Not as much now."

"You know if we swam over there together and got it, that would sure prove something to Ed and Edna, wouldn't it?" he asked.

I laughed. "Yeah, it'd sure prove *something*."

I wasn't sure exactly what. Or maybe I was simply afraid to admit what it was. Because if I was willing to jump into the frigid water, swim to the platform with him, if I was willing to risk—

"Do you trust me?" he asked quietly.

Did I?

I swallowed hard. Nodded. "Yeah, I do."

"Close your eyes, Jess."

I didn't hesitate. Not a second. Not a heartbeat. I just slid my eyes shut.

And then I felt his lips on mine. He was kissing me! And it was everything I ever thought it would be. I felt like I was falling, falling . . . but I knew that Sean would catch me. No matter how far I fell, he would be there.

He drew back. I opened my eyes.

"I'll race you to the platform," he said.

"Winner gets the banner?" I asked as I got to my feet and removed my hoodie and shorts.

"You bet," he said. "But no cheating!"

"As if I'd ever cheat," I said.

He grabbed my hand.

Laughing, we jumped off the dock . . .

Screamed as we hit the cold water . . .

And swam for the platform.

Winner takes all! I thought, knowing whether or not I beat Sean, I was still going to end up a winner.

I was in the middle of my sixth rendition of Chopin's Nocturne Opus No. 9 when a guy caught my eye as he jogged across the parking lot of the Mueller-Fordham School of Music. I stopped practicing the piano so I could watch his dark hair flutter in his face as he ran, his body lean in his jeans and T-shirt. He wasn't just cute; he was hot with an attitude. In other words: so unlike the other two hundred students at Mueller-Fordham, home of some of the geekiest musical prodigies in the greater Boston area.

After spring break, I was seriously afraid that included me. Geek, that is. Not prodigy. Not anymore.

He disappeared around the corner, and I laid my forearm across the piano keys to compare colors. My skin was the same shade as the ivory. I sighed. How could I finish my freshman year in high school like this? My arms were going to be a dead giveaway that I'd had no life this vacation.

Spending two weeks on a tour of New England with my piano teacher and six other students from the Mueller-Fordham School of Music was a form of torture that should be reserved for serial killers and people who wear ribbon barrettes.

"Good afternoon, Lily." My piano teacher, who I'd dubbed Crusty, strode into the private practice room before I could dive under the piano and hide. The rest of the world called her Miss Jespersen. Not Ms. Not Mrs. *Miss*. As in, *I'm, like, one hundred years old and still unmarried because I'm so evil that I suck the life out of any man who comes near me.*

She eyed me, as if she could see the sparkly purple toenail polish hidden under my sensible and completely unfashionable pianist-worthy shoes. I tried to breathe through my mouth, but I still caught a whiff of mothballs.

Yeah, this was the way to spend my last day

of spring break, hanging out with Miss Jespersen instead of at the pool with my friends, checking out guys. Lucky me. According to my parents, being a piano prodigy was a gift. After three years of working with Crusty, it was a gift I was ready to give back.

She waved a newspaper past my face, too quickly for me to see what it said. "You got a review from your recital in Rhode Island last weekend, along with a photo."

"Really?" I snatched the clipping from her hand, then gagged at the picture: my ugly corduroy dress with the white lace collar . . . and my nose. It looked enormous. And my bun was total old lady style. My gut sank as I saw my name in the caption beneath the photo, spelled correctly and everything. They even got my hometown of Westway, Massachusetts, correct. "What paper is this?" *Please tell me it's the monthly bulletin from the nursing home where I'd performed.*

"The Boston Globe."

"The Globe?" I croaked, horror welling over me in cold lumps of misery. "As in, circulation seventy gazillion? As in, delivered to the

3

doorstep of every single house in the state the day before school starts up again?" What if my friends saw this photo? They would totally disown me!

Miss Jespersen picked up the clipping and read from it. "With some more experience, Lily Gardner has the potential to develop into a fine musician several years down the road." She set the paper down on the piano and sighed. "Lily, we've been working too hard for you to get lackluster reviews like this. A year ago, every review proclaimed you an immediate star. Now you're reduced to having *potential*."

I bit my lower lip. "It's not as bad as my picture, at least."

"Your audition is in three weeks, but your performance has been declining over the last few months."

I felt myself tense up at the mention of that stupid audition. According to Crusty, if I didn't make it into the secondary school program at the NorthEast Seminary of Music, my piano career would be over. Forever. As would my life. This was my chance to ensure my future, and I was blowing it. If that photo hadn't destroyed my future already, of course.

Personally, I was afraid that making it *into* the program would be the final blow to my life. Starting next year, I'd have to spend four to six hours a day there after school, and all day on the weekends. My social life was bad enough now, but if I made it into the NESM program, it would be dead. The thought of never spending another minute with my friends outside of classes made me sick, and I didn't know what to do about it.

Miss Jespersen tapped the piano to get my attention. "There's no passion in your music anymore and without it, you'll fail at the audition. You don't want that, do you?"

I barely resisted the urge to cover my ears and block her out. "I'm not *trying* to fail," I said. "I'm trying to play. I'm just so tired."

"A top performer doesn't let something like exhaustion stop her." She propped the picture of freakazoid me on the piano, so I had to stare at my ugly mug. The cruelest form of torture — next to the two weeks I'd spent on tour, of course. "If I don't see some improvement in the next week, we'll need to think about holding you out of classes until the audition so you can devote yourself to—"

"No!" The only thing keeping me going was the promise of getting back to school and hanging with my friends. "I can handle school and piano, I promise." I would go insane if she made me spend 24/7 trapped in a room with her for the next three weeks. "I swear, Miss Jespersen. I can do both. I promise."

She smiled and nodded approvingly. "That's the kind of passion I like to see. Put it into your music and we won't need to talk to your mom about school."

I shuddered at the thought of her suggesting anything like that to my mom. Since Crusty had spotted me at an audition when I was eleven, my mom had fallen under her evil spell. I was my mom's chance to be the piano prodigy that she'd never managed to be. She loaded the guilt on all the time about the opportunities I had that she would have killed for, and Miss Jespersen played on that big-time. Even my dad's attempts to keep them reined in weren't always enough.

"Okay, then, let's get to work. Make the walls of this room tremble with emotion."

"Oh, sure. No problem." I stared at the sheet music, rested my fingers on the keys, and all I wanted to do was cry. Instead I lifted my chin and started to play. I could feel Crusty's disappointment after I'd played only three bars and I was about to stop when a light knock sounded on the door.

"We're in the middle of a lesson," Miss Jespersen called out.

"Come in!" I yelled at the same time, desperate for an interruption.

The door opened, and the hottie from the parking lot walked in.

Up close, he looked even better. His dark hair flopped over his left eye, his black jeans had a hole in the right knee, his T-shirt had a sweet cartoon of the band JamieX on the front of it, and there was a small tattoo peeking out from under his right sleeve. He was so not the kind of guy who belonged at the uptight

Mueller-Fordham School of Music, but here he was. Barging in on *my* piano lesson. This *rocked*.

He tossed a careless smile in our direction. "Sorry to interrupt, but I need to grab a few chairs."

Omigosh. He wasn't afraid of her at all. I sat up straighter and checked him out more closely. Who was he?

Crusty drummed her fingers on the piano top. "Just be quick, Rafe."

Rafe? Totally hot name. I bet he'd never worn a tie in his life. I sighed and leaned on the piano as he hoisted four chairs as if they weighed nothing. Cute *and* strong. And he had to be at least sixteen. And he was at *my* music school.

"Rafe? Are you coming or what?"

I jerked my head toward the door as a girl strode in. Her chest was huge, her shirt was, like, twenty sizes too small, her hair was long and highlighted, and she was gorgeous. I grabbed my photo off the piano and shoved it under my butt.

Rafe grinned at her. Not the careless smile

we'd gotten, but a real smile, one that made his green eyes crinkle. "Can you grab two music stands, Angel? I've got the rest of the stuff."

Angel? As in her real name, or as in his cute little pet name for her? I decided I didn't like her.

"Keep it quiet, please." Crusty tapped the sheet music in front of me. "Ignore them, Lily."

I gaped at her as Rafe and Angel clanged stands together, making Angel giggle and whisper to Rafe to be quiet. As if I was going to play boring classical music in front of *them*. They practically oozed attitude, and I was so not going to humiliate myself. I mean, it was bad enough that I was wearing Crusty-approved attire and was sitting on a horrific photo of myself. Playing Chopin would be a kiss of death I'd never recover from.

"Lily. Play." Crusty pinned me with a glare and I crumbled.

This was too embarrassing. *Please let him suddenly go deaf.* I felt my cheeks heat up as I started to play. Rafe glanced over at me, and my fingers stuttered. One dark eyebrow lifted, and

I forgot to keep going. I simply stared at him.

Crusty cleared her throat, and a small smile curved Rafe's lips. "Go ahead, *Lily*," he said.

"You . . . know me?" Oh, *no*. Had he seen my photo in the paper today?

"Your teacher just said your name."

Relief rushed through me and I almost felt dizzy. *He hasn't seen the picture in the* Globe.

He readjusted one of the chairs that was resting on his shoulder. "Don't let us stop you."

There was something slightly mocking in his tone, but there was something else, too. Something that made my belly go all warm and made goosebumps pop up on my arms.

"Come on, Rafe." Angel brushed past him, her shoulder intentionally knocking against his, like she wanted me to know that he was hers to touch. "Let's go."

"Right behind you." He gave me a final, speculative look that had my fingers tingling, then he turned and walked out, yanking the door shut behind him with his foot.

I sighed, then Crusty tapped my sheet music. "Play."

The warmth vanished from my body. But I started to play.

Crusty sat silent for almost a whole minute, then she shook her head and stood up. She walked out, slamming the door shut behind her.

I stared at the closed door in shock. She'd never pulled that one on me before.

She probably wanted to punish me by making me sit alone for ten minutes, contemplating all the ways that I was a failure and was letting her and my parents down.

And then I was probably supposed to start practicing so when she came back I could prove I was worthy.

I could do that. Or I could live up to my mom's constant complaints that I don't always conduct myself in a manner befitting a piano prodigy. . . .

It took me all of five seconds to grab my music off the piano, shove it in my backpack, and climb out the window.

READ ALL OF THE BOY-CRAZY BOOKS
IN THE FIRST KISSES SERIES!

First Kisses:
Trust Me

Counselor-in-training Jess finds out her trust partner is also her long-time nemesis (with beautiful blue eyes) Sean Reed, the most untrustworthy person she knows. But will Jess trust her instincts or fall in love with him anyway?

First Kisses:
The Boyfriend Trick

When the pressure of being a piano prodigy gets to be too much for Lily, her music teacher asks her to join a rock band in order to rediscover her passion. What Lily doesn't plan on is feeling passionate about Rafe, the band's drummer!

First Kisses:
Puppy Love

Allie can't wait to run a doggy day care at her mom's shop, Perfect Paws, until she has to watch over mega-snob Megan's horrible poodle, who leads her into trouble—and the arms of the boy who works at the local shelter, Jack.

First Kisses:
It Had to Be You

Fashionable, girly Emma may be an expert at giving other people romantic advice, but when it comes to boys right under her nose—like her cute next-door neighbor Kyle—Emma's completely at a loss.

First Kisses:
Playing the Field

Trisha practices soccer with this really cool sophomore Graham, a boy who finally treats her like one of the guys. But are they starting to fall for each other, or is he just playing around?

First Kisses:
The Real Thing

School photographer Hayley has a "camera crush" on football hottie Flynn, who happens to be her sister's new boyfriend. But are her feelings more than that? Could this be the real thing?

HarperTempest
An Imprint of HarperCollinsPublishers   www.harperteen.com